Tall Jerry

The Crown

TALL JERRY

AND THE

DELPHI FALLS TRILOGY

Post War
Historical Fiction
Classics

ECHOED LEGENDS

Legend Two

TALL JERRY

and the
Sideshow Pickpocket

First Edition

JEROME MARK ANTIL

ISBN-13: 978-1-7326321-8-9   (Paperback)
ISBN-13: 978-1-7326321-6-5   (Trilogy Set)

Library of Congress Control Number: 2019904864

SCENE: RURAL AMERICA
TIME: POST WAR 1953
(2 weeks after Halloween)

Historical references offered by
Judy Clancy Conway; Marty Bays; Dale Barber;
New Woodstock Historical Society; Cincinnatus
NY Historical Society; Pompey NY Historical Society; Cortland
NY Historical Society; Cazenovia Public Library; Carthage NY
Historical Society; Binghamton NY Historical Society

*This is a work of fiction. Names, characters and incidents either
are a product of the author's imagination or are used fictitiously
and any resemblance to actual persons, living or dead, business es-
tablishments, events or locales is entirely coincidental.*

Some characters are made from combinations of Jerry's siblings
(James, Paul, Richard, Frederick, Michael, Dorothy, and Mary)

TABLE OF CONTENTS

12-year-old Tall Jerry, his mom and dad. 1953

Tall Jerry in the Delphi Falls Trilogy are of a time filled with characters that show true heroism. Of legends that happened after the war and before there were cell phones and an internet, and not every house had a telephone or television. Of a time when a full, hot meal at school cost a quarter. It was a time when you could leave the house and go off to play without having to ask. The people are real, and the fictionalized legends are based in truth, give or take a stretch or two. The Delphi Falls with its shale-crusted cliffs, big white rock, my boyhood home, campsite and barn garage are there to see today if you have a mind to head on up to the town of Cazenovia, New York—near the hamlet of Delphi. Both waterfalls are magical to this day, I promise. Oh, they may not grant a wish or turn tin into gold, but they will make you feel good about yourself and give you confidence.

JMA

CHAPTER 1

BOYS WILL BE BOYS

Being a guardian angel makes my telling how a naked lady led to catching the pickpocket varmint from London awkward, if you catch my meaning. Worse, my trying to explain why ole Charlie here, a kindly guardian angel, had to up and wrench Farmer Parker's back, for a few days. Most know birds and animals can talk with angels. It was pigeons, it surely was, what helped me this time, and they began a week you won't soon forget. You're about to hear the second legend of Delphi Falls, that started, as be said, on a rafter high up in Farmer Parker's hayloft.

Ever since they moved to the Delphi Falls when Jerry was a pup, on Saturday mornings he'd often ride with Big Mike the twenty-four miles to the bakery in Homer. A mug of hot chocolate and a warm, glazed donut or two waited as a reward for walking to the post office for his dad. The bakery offices were on the second floor behind Leonard's Coffee Shop, just across the alley. He'd lift the PO drawer key from a hook on the wall and go get the mail.

The calendar that started it all with the naked lady on it had been on that coffee shop kitchen wall for some time, but fact was small Jerry was never big enough to get a full-on gander at it the other times he'd cut through the kitchen. Now he's Tall Jerry, at six foot three and with a shoe size to match his age of twelve. This morning he cut through the kitchen carrying the mail and came plunk face-to-face with the calendar. First time he laid eyes on its naked lady, Tall Jerry bolted, clanking his noggin on cooking pots hanging over the butcherblock table behind him. He grabbed his head with one

1

hand and the pots with the other to settle their clanging, turned about again, stepping in for a closer look, and this time one of his size-twelve Buster Brown shoes went under a side table and stepped on the tail of a sleeping cat.

Bolts out of the blue like this calendar girl hangin' there for the world to see could happen without warnin' to young boys in 1953, and getting stepped on, to cats of any age.

Guardian angels call them curveballs from Lucifer.

Spellbound to near stupor, the lad stood there, staring. In her full glory the lady was naked as a jaybird—and at his eye level to boot, her magnetic, blue eyes followed his eyes the way those calendar-girl eyes have a way of doing—salacious being the word.

The cat yowled a cobra-like hiss. It woke the boy, keeping him from going into a spell where he mightn't remember he had mail to deliver.

The lad gathered himself while the cat eyeballed a rip in the screen door as an opportunity when Tall Jerry might be considerate enough to lift his foot.

Turning about to see if anyone could see him gawking at the calendar lady, he took a last look and backed away. With a hiss, the cat parted company.

It was Saturday morning, around nine-thirty.

That explains things up to now.

It was a Saturday morning that would begin a week-long odyssey of a kind that could earn guardian angel wings. It's a story long since a legend in the Crown, but one that needs to be retold for the great-grandchildren. This is exactly how it began just about a week after Halloween.

The air was crisp. The leaves were bursts of reds and yellows and burnt orange as far as you could see.

Not making it easy for ole Charlie here, Tall Jerry began making inquiries that his seeing the naked lady had churned up.

Problem was he was askin' the wrong sorts. His first mistake was talkin' to his brother, Dick—known to be a scoundrel. Jerry went next to Duba—Dick's friend, and another rascal of disrepute, ready to cloud an innocence at a moment's notice.

Both were older by enough years to stir this sort of kettle to boiling. Good young men, but scamps if given opportunity to take sport in a lad's naiveté. They'd bellow foolishness, strutting about waving their arms like Gospel preachers. They were jubilant in their illustrations of seamy illusions of purposes meant for certain body

3

parts in God's creation, pausing only to watch the lad scratch his head and squirm.

A guardian angel worth a salt knows to come up with a path to alternatives, keeping moral perspective intact. If we've done our job proper, a lad could reflect on his past to find his future paths.

It's called character.

Jerry and his male friends were in the awkward stages of development. Oh, they had a healthy respect for womanhood, they truly did, but as far as birds and bees learnin' went, they was pretty much dumb as a stump.

I had good reason to want to maneuver around this Saturday morning's interruption. I'll share it in a minute, but first I'll do my best to get through Dick and Duba's braggadocios.

Struttin' around like peacocks, stompin' in the crackling leaves, they told the lad they were going to the New York State Fair in Syracuse, sneak under the tent on the Midway and sit in front-row seats to watch the breathtaking *hoochie coochie* all-girl peep show.

"What!?" Tall Jerry queried.

"It only stars *Beauteous Bombshells from a Paris Review*—least that's what the poster promises," Duba said.

"Shut up!" Jerry growled.

"Why would we waste a day gawking at a stupid wall calendar when we can see the real thing in person?" Dick asked.

"Insalubrious," Duba shouted.

"Shut up!" Jerry grunted, defending his first calendar girl.

"A bevy of ladies from the world over," Duba affirmed.

"A plethora. A virtual harem," Dick reaffirmed.

"That means a bunch," Duba offered.

Dick and Duba would punctuate inappropriate innuendo with devilish snorts, choking on cigarette smoke. They were putting on a big show in front of an innocent kid.

Normally a guardian angel would handle matters like Jerry and the calendar in due course, but adding Dick's and Duba's taunting

4

meant ole Charlie here was about to run out of time with the state fair opening this week. I had to think.

I remembered my flock borrowed Farmer Parker's hay fork-lift on Halloween to hoist Conway and the two girls up top of the tree the night they caught the POW escapees. That hay forklift got me thinking. I knew Tall Jerry needed distraction from Dick and Duba's talk of calendar girls and girlie-girl shows, so I would have me a talk with some pigeons, and I'd see to it the ole man wasn't hurt permanent at the same time.

It happens that Farmer Parker got laid up a few days when he reached off his tall barn ladder trying to rehang the forklift to the top of his hayloft cupola.

That was just what I needed. The flock of pigeons fluttered from a rafter, spookin' him and causin' him to lose footing, but with my help he caught himself, with a slight wrenching of his back. It was slight, but a wrenching it was, and Dr. Brudny came in from Ridge Road shakin' a finger at him for trying to climb such a tall ladder at his age and ordered him three days bed rest.

A flock of pigeons setting up in a barn's hayloft stirred a distraction in 1953, and the second legend of Delphi Falls had begun.

"Mrs. Parker, make this geezer lie still and get this here liniment applied—like it or not—every few hours," the doctor said.

Well, pained as he was, Farmer Parker was a-grinnin' and snickerin' a mite into his pillow. Had been since the night he helped run those POW escapees off to their just desserts—making him feel young and alive again.

Thing was, here in the Crown, *bed* and *rest* were two words that didn't often appear together in a farmer's vocabulary. Least not in 1953 they didn't. They couldn't. Cows had to be milked twice a day—before sunup and after sundown. Manure had to be spread, and even though the sun was good on the field for now, he couldn't take a chance on rain coming. The cut hay on top of the hill looking down over the cemetery had to be barn-lofted before rain tainted it in the field, leaching out its nutrition.

Thinking all what had to be done and nobody to do it was when Mrs. Parker set her cup and saucer down and picked the wall telephone earpiece from its cradle. She cranked the handle and asked Myrtie, the operator, if she would kindly get Missus, across the way, on the wire. She then proceeded to tell Missus their woes, holding back the weepy tears of despair in her tone.

Mrs. Parker was a strong woman. Farm women were—like the roses behind her porch she raised mainly on supper dishwater. She just needed a good ear for now and maybe some ideas—some time to think.

"Fay doesn't cotton to being laid up," she said. "Worse, he says he won't be still. He's determined to work the farm."

"No husband does," Missus said. "Like to stay put. They're such boys when they're sick."

"I'm afraid he'll hurt himself permanently," Mrs. Parker said. "Without this farm, I don't know what we'd do."

"Now don't you worry, dear," Missus said. "There're plenty of friends around to help. Let me find my boys, and I'll call you back. No need to fret. Sit by the phone."

Before hanging up, Mrs. Parker added, "He's worried because the almanac says a rough winter is coming."

Missus walked through the house looking for either Jerry or Dick. Their brother, Gourmet Mike, was away at college. This being a Saturday neither were to be found. No telling where they were off to but, in her mind, Dick was most likely with Duba under the hood of a car somewhere. Jerry, she thought, was probably back from his Saturday morning trip to the bakery with Big Mike and up under the second falls with Holbrook, plinking cans with the .22, or above it, watching beavers build a dam for winter.

Not certain, Missus picked up the phone.

"Myrtie, can you connect me with the Barbers, please?"

"Are you looking for your boys, Missus?"

"Desperately! The Parkers need help."

"I've heard," Myrtie said.

"I need to find either of them."

If any one person could thread a needle of where every living soul was in the Crown in 1953, it was the rural telephone operator out of New Woodstock. From her second-floor walk-up telephone exchange board Myrtie could smell a trail of anyone who's picked up a telephone better than a bloodhound. She'd even been known to help the club solve a crime or two by using her talent for listening.

"Dick called for Duba this morning to meet him in Manlius for something or other. It seems to me it was about getting car parts—spark plugs or something," Myrtie said.

She spared Missus from what else she learned listening in on Dick and Duba's conversation—their going on about wondering if they'd get seen by any teachers or caught by any parents when they sneak into the "girlie-girlie" show tent this coming Friday at the state fair.

"They were both going to drive and meet up in Manlius," Myrtie said. "Jerry's at Barbers, helping shovel manure into the honey wagon. Big Mike dropped him there not long ago. According to Tommy Kellish this morning up on Berry Road, Holbrook isn't working at the Tully bakery today and is being dropped off at Barber's as soon as Mr. Holbrook comes home from the railroad and can drive him. He would have walked, but he had to hang wash on the clothesline for his mother. They're going to a picture show in Cazenovia. Jerry with the money Mr. Barber pays him for shovelling manure."

Myrtie took a deep breath.

Young Bobby answered, "Hello?"

"Here you go, Missus, good luck," Myrtie interrupted. "If I hear anything, I'll ring you."

"Hello, I'm looking for Dale. To whom am I speaking, please?"

"Hi Missus, this is Bobby."

"Bobby, it's good to hear your voice. Hello, and how's your father?"

"Daddy's good. They're putting up silage today."

"Tell him hello for us."

"I will. Dale's in the barn with Tall Jerry."

"Sweetheart, would you please run out and get Jerry and put him on?"

"Hold on, I'll get him."

"Thank you, dear."

While she waited, Missus thought of Mrs. Parker's plight, a farm with no hired help, in need of a helping hand. She knew Jerry and others would be there for him.

She thought back to the time (not that long ago) her Big Mike was taken away for a year with tuberculosis.

Dick and Jerry had stepped off the school bus and saw a car they didn't recognize driving toward them from the house, crunching down the ice-crusted, snowy drive…they could tell by the stature of the silhouette they were able to make out that Big Mike was in the back seat, a passenger. Big Mike's tests had come back positive for TB, and they were afraid the boys could be infected, so they drove on. The car didn't stop or even so much as slow down for the boys to get a look.

Thinking back to that day Missus remembered that Jerry started to cry. Like he cried when ole Charlie here died. Their dad had never left the family like this before and neither of the boys had any idea why—or why he didn't stop to talk. That's how Jerry and Dick learned their dad had tuberculosis and they wouldn't be able to see him for the year and few months he would be in a "sanatorium."

"He and his brother Dick took charge and ran the house while their dad was away," Missus said to herself. Jerry wouldn't let his friend down, she thought; it wasn't in his nature.

Hearing sounds of footsteps coming through the earpiece, Missus started from her daydream, sitting up straight.

"Hello?"

"Jerry, Farmer Parker is hurt. He needs help."

Click.

It wasn't but forty-five minutes when Tall Jerry, Barber, and Bases were standing on the gray back porch talking with Mrs. Parker about all there was to get done. In another hour Randy's pap, Carl Vaas, dropped Randy, Holbrook, Mary, and the Mayor off to help.

Things were going to happen.

Tall Jerry and his friends were about to get it done for Farmer Parker. A friend was in need.

A legend was beginning to unfold. A legend you won't soon be forgetting.

Big Mike's and Missus's house and Delphi Falls.

CHAPTER 2

LIFT THAT CAN, TOTE THAT PAIL

For a Border Collie, Buddy was gettin' on in years. 'Bout blind with cataracts, but he surely knew Farmer Parker's young friend by scent and gentle manner. He missed Tall Jerry but hadn't stepped off the back porch to run greet him like in the old days for more than a year.

Tall Jerry steered the book club with a jerking head motion down toward the barn. The old dog lumbered off the porch and followed alongside, nudgin' the lad's leg as if it was his compass.

Doc Webb turned onto the drive, and he and Mrs. Webb stepped out of his jeep. Catching Jerry's and Mary's eye, the doc waved a thumbs-up in the group's direction, clasping hands and wriggling them over his head like a boxer in congratulations for running off the Nazi crooks.

"Bully for you!" he bellowed his Teddy Roosevelt yell.

Halloween was still the talk in the Crown and promising to be for some time to come.

"We have potato salad," Mrs. Webb said. "Hope you like mustard. We have pickled beets and a dish of apple-crumb bake as well."

"Bless my soul," Mrs. Parker said from the porch. "Will you be taking a jar of my butter pickles back with you? I was hoping to enter them at the fair, but now I don't know. I have plenty, please take a jar home."

"We will, thank you. The apple-crumb is from the Butlers—best in the county—and the pickled beets are from the Chubbs," Mrs. Webb said.

"More is coming," the doc said. "Now if you or Fay don't like apple-crumb declare now, and I will personally take it off your hands."

"Oh, Doc—now hush!" Mrs. Webb chided.

"You concentrate on getting that fuddy-duddy back on his feet, Mrs. P. Let your friends keep you out of kitchen chores for a spell," the doc said.

Jerry, Buddy, and the others stepped around to the side door of the barn. By the time they'd pulled the door open and found the light switches, more cars had dropped off dishes, baked goods, and well wishes before heading back to their own chores. Big Mike stopped to pass the word to the helpers in the barn that he was making spaghetti for whenever they were done. They would hold supper for them. He didn't know Missus had already announced it to the lad when she walked a basket of Moore's farm apples over to Mrs. Parker.

Club president Mary took charge.

"Tell us what to do, Tall Jerry," she said.

"What?" Jerry asked.

"You know this barn and farm better than any of us, and you've talked with Mrs. Parker. Tell us what to do."

Jerry bent down and scratched under Buddy's collar, letting the dog know he was a remembered friend, and they appreciated him being there. He knelt and moved a pail from the concrete ledge Buddy was used to sleeping on while Farmer Parker milked. He lifted the dog onto it and let him "nest-sniff" around a circle or two to settle in. Maybe he'd take a nap.

"Okay," Jerry said.

He looked around the barn, jogging his memory.

"Holbrook, reach up and switch on the radio. Cows like music."

He pointed to a ladder built onto a wall in front of a cow stall.

"After that, go up and pitch hay down the chute. Mary and I will put it in front of the milking stalls. Pile it up under the chute."

"Okay," Holbrook said.

"What we don't use tonight we can use in the morning."

"Barber, you and Mayor get the milking machines hooked up and ready. There should be two of them. You guys know."

Barber and Mayor stepped toward the cabinet where the milking machines were stored.

"I know cows are stripped by hand after the machine comes off," Jerry said. "Will you guys need help stripping after you take the machines off?"

"We can strip them, no problem," Mayor said. "But with the two of us working them, we'll need two milk pails. Somebody taking the full pails and hauling them over and pouring them through the strainer and fetching them back to us for the next cow."

"Like a production line," Mary said.

"It can help make it go faster," Barber said.

Everyone nodded they would be watchful and grab the full milk pails, walk them to the cans for pouring through the strainers, and return them to Barber or Mayor empty.

"Randy, find the filter cloths and set up the funnels we'll need to strain the milk into the milk cans—and then can you put a scoop of silage in the manger in front of each stall?" Jerry asked.

"Sure can," Randy said.

"Bases, organize the milk cans, try to line them up, make sure they're clean for Randy."

"Will do," Bases said.

"It's colder after sunset, so if you can watch for the cows to come down the driveway when Mary and I call them in we won't lose heat in the barn if you slide that end barn door open wide for them to come in and close it behind. The cow's body heat will warm it up. They'll know their stalls," Jerry said.

Mary, we'll go call the cows—and then we'll put the hay in front of their stalls."

"I'm impressed," Barber said, while rigging a machine to the teat cups. "Not half bad for a city boy."

"Can you guys be here in the morning to do this all over again?" Jerry asked. "Tomorrow we have to shovel manure into the spreader after the morning milking."

"Morning comes early on a farm, Tall Jerry. Can we stay over at your place?" Barber asked.

"It's already arranged. My mom said yes to your staying over and called your parents. She called the principal, too. He said if Farmer Parker is still laid up on Monday, we don't have to go to school so long as we're here, so we won't be marked absent or tardy."

"Perfect," Mary said.

"My dad's making spaghetti for whenever we get our work done here."

"Meatballs?" Barber asked.

"He makes meatballs and sausage and Italian garlic bread."

"Yahoo," Holbrook shouted while hanging from the hay chute's wall ladder.

Jerry and Mary stepped out of the barn and walked up the cinder drive toward the road.

"Did you ever think we'd be running a farm, even if it's only for a day or so?" Mary asked.

"I'm worried about the hay," Jerry said.

"What's to worry? Didn't you say there's a chute from the hayloft Holbrook can drop it through?"

"I mean in the field on top of the hill—the hay that's been cut," Jerry said. He pointed at the tallest hill on the back side of the place.

"That hill—it's the same one that overlooks the cemetery on the other side. I climb it to come home from our meetings."

"It's already cut?" Mary asked.

14

"The thing is I don't know how to hitch anything up—like the horses, the hay lift, or the hay wagon—and we have to get the hay down into the barn before it rains, or it'll spoil."

"Seems you knew what needed to be done for milking," Mary said. "Who'd-a-thunk that?"

"I've seen Farmer Parker do his milking a million times."

"How about the music to make happy cows? I didn't know that one," Mary said.

"I don't want Farmer Parker worrying about the hay," Jerry said.

"I'm sure you'll figure out the hay thing. Someone will help us," Mary said.

Mary crossed the road and opened the barbed wire fencing at the base of the side pasture hill, pulling it back and out of the way.

Jerry rubbed his hands together to warm them in the dusk air. He cupped them into a megaphone over his mouth and copied Farmer Parker's cow call as best he could:

"Cahobosse! Cahobosse! Cahobosse!"

(Come Home Bossy!)

He paused and looked up the hill.

"Cahobosse! Cahobosse! Cahobosse!"

Wasn't long before Tall Jerry and Mary saw the Holstein heads appear way up the hill, bobbing up and down, up and down, back and forth, as the cows lined up single file and made their way down the steep, warn, cow path, around the briar bushes. The cows pretty much knew Tall Jerry by now. They seemed contented. Step-by-step they came through the gate, nostrils snorting steam. They crossed the road, looking forward to being milked, and to a manger of oats. Jerry waved a signal to Bases to pull the door open and the cows headed down the cinder drive and through the back door and into their own stalls.

"Let's count them, Mary. Let's make sure they're all in and we didn't leave any up on the hill," Jerry said.

15

Ole Charlie here was busting my buttons watching the goins' on. Reminded me of the time young Jerry asked his brother, Gourmet Mike, when his mother would let him go out with girls, like to the picture show or to a school dance.

"Probably when you don't have to ask," was the answer Gourmet Mike gave him—and it was a good one.

Watching these young folks here—they ain't just milking cows or pitching hay or cleaning and filling milk pails. If someone was to ask a guardian angel to describe when a boy becomes a man and when a girl becomes a woman, I'd say this was about it. They were on the mountain tonight. I'd have to say full-grown the minute they didn't bother to ask—not a one had to ask—to step up and help. Put a happy tear in my soul, it surely did.

The chores done, pails and milking machines cleaned proper, Jerry told them to go to the hen house and use the garden hose to freshen up and then to head on over to the house across the way. He'd be along for supper after he gave a report to the Parkers and told them that they'd be back in the morning.

"You go on, I'll get the lights," Jerry said.

With the barn empty, he stood in the middle and took it in, slowly turning a full circle. The cows were quiet for the most part. Contented they were milked and staying in the barn overnight out of the cold. He thought back to the first time he came into the barn when he was nine. It was an autumn chill like tonight. He chuckled to himself about his first episode with his getting behind Farmer Parker's manure spreader—and that tomorrow he'd be certain to stay in front of it. He walked over to get Buddy and turn off the lights.

"Let's go, Buddy."

Buddy didn't move when Jerry called. He didn't stand and stretch like the boy was used to seeing him wake up.

He felt the dog's heart, then sat down on the ledge beside him and scratched under his collar one last time. He pursed his lips and looked up on the wall at an emptiness of the moment, trying to get his mind around it, thinking what to do. There was a wall calendar with a picture of a Ford tractor.

"Farmer Parker always said when the horses, Sarge and Sally, give out he was going to get him a Ford tractor," he whispered to Buddy.

He remembered that and the calendar in Homer and of Dick and Duba going on about sneaking in under a tent at the state fair.

Somehow tonight—in a moment like this—life didn't seem to be about sneaking in to Tall Jerry. Life was about leaving, as well.

"Mrs. Parker, is Farmer Parker still up?"

"Come in Jerry. He'd love to see you, come on in, dear."

Farmer Parker was resting back on two pillows. A rolled-up newspaper was in his hand, watchful under the bedside lamp for a bothersome housefly.

"Son, I can't thank you enough. Your friends are good people."

"We're your friends, too, Farmer Parker."

"We'll have to do something special when I'm up on my feet again."

"Farmer Parker, there's something I've got to tell you."

"How'd the milking go? All right? Find everything you needed?"

"We found it. It's all clean and put away," Jerry said. "We hosed it down good."

"Maybe we'll have a cookout," Farmer Parker said.

"In the morning we're putting the cans out for Mr. Vaas to pick up after milking. Barber and Mayor are good with the milking machines. We're lucky."

18

"Maybe a hayride."

"Buddy died."

The man's shoulders slumped.

"Sure enough?" He looked up at the ceiling, raised his fists, gently tapping them to his mouth.

"Buddy followed me down to the barn; I set him up on the ledge he liked. I'm sorry if…"

"Now that was one good ole dog. A friend if there ever was one. He'd wear himself thin running up that side pasture hill getting the cows down and into the barn."

"I know," Jerry said.

"That's right, you've seen him do it. Gave them fits, didn't he?"

Jerry was silent.

"He surely did," Farmer Parker whispered. "Kept them in tow. A good ole dog he surely was—Buddy."

"What do you want me to do with him?" Jerry asked.

Farmer Parker looked over at Mrs. Parker standing in the doorway, then he looked back at Jerry.

"Where is he?"

"He's lying on the ledge in the barn."

"He loves that ledge," Farmer Parker said.

"I left the lights on out of respect until I talked with you."

Farmer Parker pulled on his bushy eyebrows thinking, then he looked over at Mrs. Parker, still standing in the shadow of the bedroom door, wiping her eyes with a hanky.

"Are the cows in pasture or in the barn?" the old man asked.

"We're keeping them in the barn tonight because of the cold. It'll make it easier than calling them in the dark in the morning."

"Ole Buddy surely needed the rest," Farmer Parker said.

"He was a good dog," Tall Jerry said.

"Let's let him be tonight. Let him get a good night's rest on his favorite spot, with his friends," Mrs. Parker said.

19

"Go ahead and turn the lights out, son," the old man said. "I'll have an idea where you might put him in the morning. Come ask me after milking."

"I'm sorry, Farmer Parker. Buddy was a good dog."

"Thank you, son, and thanks for taking Buddy with you to the barn. He loved that old barn—couldn't have been a better place in the world for him to pass."

"I'm sorry," Jerry said.

"Night, son."

"Good night."

Jerry stepped away.

"Tall Jerry?"

He turned.

"Yes, sir?"

"Why not let's leave the radio on for Buddy tonight?"

"Okay."

"He likes to hear the music and Deacon Doubleday's early morning farm report. Calms him."

CHAPTER 3

DYING IS A PART OF GROWING UP

Missus welcomed the crew to the table, told them where to sit—Mary, Bases, Randy, Barber, Holbrook, Tall Jerry, Mayor, and Dick—and then started supper with a prayer.

"Bless us, oh Lord, and these thy gifts for which we are about to receive from thy bounty through Christ our Lord. Amen."

"Buddy died," Jerry said.

Smiles froze as they looked at the lad.

"I already told Farmer Parker."

"When did he…?" Mary whimpered.

"He died in his sleep down in the barn."

"While we were there?" Randy asked.

"Yes," Jerry said.

"How'd he take it? His dying," Randy asked.

"He was an old dog. I think Farmer Parker's been expecting it, but he was still sad," Jerry said.

"Like when Charlie Pitts died," Holbrook said. "We knew he had cancer, but we were still sad when he died."

"At least Buddy wasn't alone when he died," Randy said. "Shouldn't anyone ever die alone, like Charlie did."

"Charlie knows we love him. We meet in the cemetery by his stone," Mary said.

If they only knew, ole Charlie here never was alone. They was there, the instant I died, me being their guardian angel.

"Buddy was my pal," Jerry said. "Even blind, he followed me to the barn."

"Buddy was in heaven," Barber said.

"Was? You mean now he *is* in heaven, like he went to heaven," Holbrook said.

"No," Barber said. "He *was* in heaven. Some animals, dogs for sure, pick their heaven and go there before they die."

"Is that true?" Holbrook asked.

"I heard elephants do," Randy said.

"If you believe folklore," Mayor said. "My ancestors came over as pilgrims. I think they believed animals went to their heaven before they died, so they could know their surroundings and rest easier."

"You saying Buddy's heaven was watching his cows being milked?" Mary asked.

"He liked listening to the music in the barn," Jerry said.

"Folks, let's pass the spaghetti bowl, the sauce, and the meat platter before it gets cold," Big Mike said.

"I think what you're doing is admirable," Missus said. "Stepping up to help the Parkers. Isn't that right, dear?"

Missus looked down at Big Mike.

He was remembering his boys running the house and doing chores while he was gone to the TB sanitorium. Now his boy and his friends were there for the Parkers.

"How did Farmer Parker get hurt?" Randy asked.

"He slipped on a ladder—wrenched his back," Missus said.

Hearing about the ladder, Jerry started. "My grandfather fell off a barn roof, didn't he, Dad?"

The words choked the lad as the second he had them out of his mouth he remembered his mother telling him what a sensitive subject that was for Big Mike.

"That was a difficult time," Missus said. "It happened when Jerry's father was about your ages. Mike, aren't you proud of these young ones for being there for the Parkers?"

Mike set his fork down and unclenched his lips.

"My dad was paralyzed in a hospital bed for a year before he went. I quit school to earn money to help my mother. I wanted to see him, but we didn't have a car, and it was too far to walk to St. Paul."

"Like the time you were in the TB sanatorium and I couldn't see you for the whole year," Jerry said.

The phone rang.

"I'll get it," Jerry said, interrupting his thought.

The distraction helped Big Mike hold back a tear.

Jerry stood and went into his mom and dad's bedroom to answer it. In a few minutes he returned and sitting down he looked over at Mary. She puffed a curl from over her eye.

"That was Marty. He knows how to hay it and is riding over in the morning to help us out."

"My dad would bring him when he's making his route," Randy said.

"He's riding his horse," Jerry said.

The clatter of spoons in bowls and forks on platters with the sounds of the waterfalls in back filled the room. It was after the first bite of warm food and spaghetti sauce when the book club remembered what enormous appetites they'd worked up. Missus looked about at the happy faces and gave reprieve, making no notice of table manners. She set 'em aside for this supper, figured she could give the table linen a good soaking tonight and wash it in the morning.

"Jerry, do you remember the night I came home after that year of being away in the sanatorium?" Big Mike asked.

The table got so quiet you could hear a thought. Every soul sittin' there wanted to hear a story, and they knew Big Mike was the best at telling them.

"I remember," Jerry said softly.

Big Mike sat back, looked around the table.

23

"It was Christmas Eve. In the time I was gone, Jerry had grown from the boy who used to ride with me to the bakery into our Tall Jerry here, almost a foot taller than when I went in. Jerry didn't know his mom had told me how he'd grown—and he was afraid I wouldn't recognize him, shooting up the way he had…the way you all had."

His friends looked at Jerry. They could remember members of their family being away at the war for years and coming home, everyone changed.

"It was a cold winter night; a snow storm was becoming flurries. A medical aid was driving me home from the sanatorium, and we stopped at Shea's store to scrape ice off the windshield. Mike Shea called here and told how close I was to being home for the first time in more than a year. You remember what you did when you heard, Jerry?"

"Yes," Jerry said, pursing his lips.

"Jerry jumped off the front step barefoot in his pajamas, running through the snow toward the front gate, not taking his eyes off the top of the road up by Farmer Parker's hill. He was looking for headlights from the car I'd be in. Finally, he saw some, and our car came slowly over the snowy hill, inching down around the curve. We turned into the driveway and paused. I rolled the back window down and stuck out my hand for a shake. Jerry's eyes widened. He grabbed my hand walking alongside as we drove in. Why I knew Jerry-me-boy right off. I was speechless, so happy to see him again. 'Jerry?' I asked. I guess I said it like I wasn't sure, but I was sure. He grimaced a sad look. You see, growing that much since I saw him last, Jerry wasn't sure I'd recognize him. It frightened him. He started rambling—to jog my memory—while following the car holding on to my hand. Things like, 'Remember fishing at Little York Lake? Remember I rowed us out in the boat at Sandy Pond? Remember when you beat my airplane to Watertown? Remember teaching me how to make desserts? Can you remember me, Dad?'

24

We were close to the house and the family was on the porch waving and cheering. I shook Jerry me-boy's hand and said…You remember what I said, Jerry?"

"Yes."

"I said: 'You caught the croppies we cooked at the Imperial House. Remember, son?"

"'Room number six, Dad,' you said back."

"'Room number six,' I answered. That was the room we would stay in at the Imperial Hotel in Carthage. It showed Jerry I remembered him. When I got out of the car and stood up straight, I looked at Jerry and how tall he'd grown. Jerry didn't know I was as afraid that he wouldn't know me with gray hair after a year away and being operated on. Son, I'll never forget what you said. You stood tall and looked me in the eye and said, 'I'm still the same, Dad—just like you're still the same.'"

Big Mike looked around the table. He choked up and looked down at his plate and fumbled for his fork.

"That was beautiful. Tall Jerry, did you run out in the snow barefoot?" Mary asked.

The lad nodded.

"That was a nice story," Holbrook said.

"There's a reason I wanted to tell it," Big Mike said. "I think you should know how filled your lives are going to be down the road for helping Farmer Parker like this. The man will never forget it for as long as he lives."

Missus knew Big Mike needed a moment.

"Mary, you're sleeping in Mike's room. He's at LeMoyne. Boys, you work out sleeping arrangements. There're plenty of blankets and pillows in the hall closet. I'll set an alarm and wake you."

"At five?" Barber asked.

"Five is fine," Missus said.

Mary leaned over to Missus. "I got my records in the mail. On Wednesday I was going to have a social for friends. If we're still helping the Parkers on Wednesday, do you think maybe I should cancel it?"

"If there are things to do, chores at the Parker's should be over about the same time as tonight, dear. I don't see why there wouldn't be time for a party," Missus said. "I know you'll have the energy."

"I have new square-dance records. Will you guys come?"

Mouths full, the lads around the table nodded they would be there.

"We'll see that you all have rides to Mary's house and back here after the dance," Missus said.

"There'd better be girls there to dance with," Holbrook said.

"The bakery is giving anybody who helps the Parkers tickets to the state fair," Big Mike said.

"That's nice, thank you," Mary said.

"Dick here can take you to the fair on Friday when he goes. Dick, you'll get a ticket and gas money for driving them."

"But I'm going with Duba. I can't fit them," Dick said.

"Good," Big Mike said. "You and Duba can both drive. There'll be plenty of room in two cars."

Dick moaned.

"Bring them home, too. You have to plan a time to meet up somewhere on the fair grounds to load up and come home."

"We'll meet on the Midway," Jerry snickered, knowing what Dick and Duba were up to.

"Maybe we can meet at the shooting range," Holbrook said.

Dick stabbed a meatball with his fork and snarled.

CHAPTER 4

SMALL TALK OF NAKED LADIES

Boxes of breakfast cereal, a bowl of bananas and a pitcher of milk were on the kitchen counter when Missus woke everyone at five. Barber walked in rubbing his eyes.

"We appreciate it," Barber said, pulling a sweater over his head, "but on a farm we have to do the milking before breakfast."

"Why's that?" Mary asked as she walked in.

"It can be painful if their sacks aren't emptied twice a day on a regular basis. Then we put them out to pasture to graze and chew their cuds," Barber said.

"No grazing, no milk," Mayor said.

"After milking's done and we've loaded the spreader is when we can eat before we go back to work," Barber said.

It was a dark, star-clouded morning outside. They stepped from the house and walked the long gravel drive to the gate. They crossed the road and took the shortcut on the north side of Parker's house, filing up over the yard. Mrs. Parker was waiting for them on the back porch.

"Come in for breakfast after milking."

"My mom has cereal for us," Jerry said.

"Nonsense, I'll call her. I'll have a hot breakfast waiting for you."

Randy found the barn's light switch. They stepped in and gathered about Buddy, layin' there peaceful like, tuckered from an active, happy life, cataract eyes glazed over. Mary petted him on the head.

The morning farm report with Deacon Doubleday was on the radio, bringing the barn to life.

"Good morning folks—this is the Deacon speakin' from the wired woodshed.

Only man in the great northeast wired for sight and sound.

Stay tuned for early crop reports, the weather and a look at the humididdy and all the news that'll get you through the day by starting off on the right foot."

"Maybe we should turn the radio down," Mary said.

"I think we're supposed to say something nice for Buddy, aren't we?" Randy asked.

"Don't we do that when we bury him?" Mayor asked.

"He likes the radio," Jerry said.

"Let's do it after we finish the chores," Holbrook said.

"Do what?" Mary asked.

"Bury him or say the prayers and stuff."

"Holbrook's right," Jerry said. "Getting work done for his master is what Buddy would want more than anything."

"Holbrook's right," Bases said.

"Did you guys use strip cups last night when you milked?" Jerry asked.

"Why you askin'?" Barber asked.

"What do you know about strip cups?" Mayor asked.

"Marty told me to make sure we use strip cups when we milk is all. I don't know why," Jerry said.

"Where was Marty last night come milking time?" Mayor barked. "He wanting to run the show from Ridge Road now, is he?"

"He didn't mean anything by it," Jerry said. "He's coming to hay it. That'll take most of the day. Cut him some slack."

"What's a strip cup?" Mary asked.

Barber reached under his shirttail and pulled one he'd tied to his belt and held it up.

"This is a strip cup," Barber said.

"What's it for?" Jerry asked.

"A cow's milk sack is divided into quarters. Four quarters, four teats. If a quarter gets bruised a cow can get mastitis in the quarter that got hurt. If the strip cup says there's mastitis in the milk from that quarter, it all has to be thrown away."

"Good," Jerry said. "So you used one."

"Nah," Barber sneered. "I like to carry it for showing off to the girls."

"Yeah," Mayor said. "I used Farmer Parker's strip cup here to hold my pencils."

"Simmer down, all of you," Mary said.

"Barber and Mayor are as good as anybody can get in a dairy barn," Randy said. "That's what my dad would say."

"Jerry doesn't know about farming, guys," Mary said. "It was good he asked."

"I was only asking," Jerry said.

"Give him a break," Mary said.

"Well, make sure you remind Marty the hay is that green stuff laying on top of the back hill," Barber snapped. "And a pitchfork is—"

"Enough!" Mary said.

"Let's get to work," Bases said.

"We sure gave Buddy a show, acting like jerks. What a send-off," Holbrook said.

"Somebody tell a joke," Mary said.

"I don't know any jokes," Bases said.

"Okay, so why don't cows have any money on them?" Randy asked.

"I give up. Why?" Holbrook asked.

"Because farmers milk them dry."

It would take more than a ripple to rattle this club for long, even a bad joke. Morning chores flowed smooth as butter, the milking machine suction cups clicking and ticking like a wind-up clock. Jerry, Holbrook, Bases, and Randy pushed the end door aside and rolled the spreader into the barn by turning on the spokes of its iron wheels. They shoveled manure from gutters and moved it forward to shovel more. Once the spreader was filled, and the gutters behind the cows emptied, they rolled it outside. They met up at the house for breakfast.

"Mrs. Parker, is there any more bacon?" Randy asked.

"Why, young man, a body'd swear you had a tapeworm," Mrs. Parker said. "Plenty of bacon, dear—help yourself."

"Mrs. Parker, did you ever teach at the Delphi one-room schoolhouse when it was going?" Barber asked.

"I did."

"Is it true that each row of desks was a different grade and you taught everybody all at once?" Mary asked.

"That's how it was, and I probably taught most of your parents a time or two," Mrs. Parker said.

"Do you know any secrets we can blackmail them with?" Mayor asked.

Mrs. Parker smiled and looked out the back window. She saw Marty riding in the drive on Sandy, his palomino. She opened the back door and waved at him to bring the horse up on the lawn and hitch him to the porch railing.

"That pretty horse can't do the lawn any harm grazing, and with luck my roses will get some lasting benefit."

They gathered around on the back porch, some with bacon in their hands.

"I see the cows on the hill. Looks like you got through the milking," Marty said.

"We haven't done anything with Sarge or Sally, the workhorses," Jerry said. "They've been in the pasture all night. Do we need to do anything for them?"

They stepped off the back porch and started toward the barn.

"A bucket of oats and let them share it will be all you need. They'll use the drum trough for water," Marty said.

"I'll get the oats and feed them," Mary said.

"Is the hill out back the only one with cut hay on it?" Marty asked.

"Yes," Jerry said.

"Do you know when he cut it?"

"We think a few days ago. Before he hurt his back."

"Has it been raked?"

"I'm pretty sure," Jerry said. "Rows of hay that look like big long roles of carpet line the length of the field."

"Then it's been raked."

"Not sure when, though. If it's important, I'll run back up and ask Farmer Parker."

"Nah, we're good. We'll get it in today," Marty said.

"Let us know what we can do," Holbrook said.

"I'll need two with me on the hay wagon. Well, three of you with one as a lookout."

"A lookout? For what? Indians?" Holbrook snorted.

"I'll be tending a team of horses I don't know. We'll be pulling a wagon I don't know, and that's pulling a hay-lift rig I've never seen or used before," Marty said.

"Let's get serious, guys," Mary said.

"I'll need another set of eyes watching out for things," Marty said.

"Name it," Mayor said.

"Two with hay forks pitching the hay around, even on the wagon. The hay-lifter rig will pick it off the field and drop it," Marty said.

Marty scratched his head. "After we get the hay in the barn, "somebody can hitch the team up to the spreader, but if it were me, I'd let them rest and spread tomorrow after the morning milking."

"I'll take the honey wagon up in the morning," Barber said.

"I saw a rope hanging from the cupola, but I didn't see a hay-fork lift," Marty said.

31

"Farmer Parker never got it put back up before he hurt himself," Jerry said.

"I'll get it hung," Holbrook said. "Randy can help. I've seen him use it. I'm pretty sure I know how it works."

"If the ropes are all up there and ready, we'll be good," Randy said.

"Try testing it with a bag of corn husks," Marty said. "Make sure it connects to the rail at the top. You'll hear a click. Then it should roll on the rail into the barn over toward the center. Try pulling the rope to see if it'll release and drop the bag."

Barber and Mayor appreciated Marty's knowledge of horses. They both worked family farms where hay was baled by machines. They had tractors to work with. Handling hay with hay-lifts, hay-forks and a team of horses was foreign to them. It was time-consuming and back-breaking farming, but that was farming in much of the Crown.

They stepped out of the barn to help Marty hitch up the team to the hay wagon. Jerry ran back up to the house and climbed the stairs to say hello to Farmer Parker.

"We're going to get the hay put in the barn today," Jerry said. "Marty knows how."

"Appreciate it, son," Farmer Parker said.

"Have you thought more about what you want us to do with Buddy?"

"I was thinking most the night how much he loved running to the top of the pasture hill across the road when it was cow-calling time."

"I remember," Jerry said.

"Most always around sunset. It'd give him pleasure—stubby as his legs were—making it all the way to the top before some of the cows even had a chance to stand up."

"I remember," Jerry said.

"Son, you suppose your friends could see to it Buddy gets buried somewhere on top of that hill?"

"We can do that, no problem," Jerry said.

"See you put him in the sun directly. Buddy loved the sun."

"We'll do it this afternoon."

"The sun is hottest at three," Farmer Parker said.

"We'll find a good sunny spot and do it around then or when we get off the hayfield," Jerry said.

"Say some words, too," Farmer Parker said.

"Mary is good at that—saying words."

"Bring me his collar, son."

"Sure."

Farmer Parker handed the lad a grapefruit-size rock.

"And put this on his grave."

"A rock?" Jerry asked.

"This was the first stone I ever pulled from the hayfield when I was making it ready for plowing. Buddy will remember it and appreciate the company."

Jerry carried the rock down to the barn and set it next to Buddy on the ledge.

Marty had Sarge and Sally hitched up to the hay wagon. He stood between the horses, tightening buckles. The wagon was ready for the long haul up the steep hill to the hayfield.

Holbrook and Randy were working on hooking the hay fork up in the hayloft cupola.

Mary and Mayor were walking up the hill carrying a bucket of drinking water and ladle.

"Pull her up some, Marty, and I'll close the gate behind the wagon," Jerry said.

Stepping up on the hay wagon and sitting on its bench, Marty looked behind him and noticed his horse, Sandy, had dropped a fresh pile of fertilizer as a courtesy for Mrs. Parker's red roses.

"Yo, Holbrook? Randy?" he shouted.

No answer.

He finally got Holbrook's attention with a two finger-in-the-lip whistle.

"When you get down off that ladder, can ya put Sandy in the back pasture?"

Randy waved okay.

"Put the saddle and bridle up off the ground where they won't get peed on."

Jerry clamped the gate closed and climbed on the wooden seat bench.

Marty lifted and lowered the reins with a gentle slap on the rumps of Sarge and Sally.

"Ktch, Ktch," Marty crackled. "Let's go, hosses—giddyap!"

Leather stretched and squeaked; chains tinkled and rattled; wood creaked as iron-trimmed wagon wheels started rolling over the pebbles and dusty powder of the trail.

The wagon made its way down the slope. With a clunk, clunk, clunk, clunk sound of hooves, it crossed over the back creek's wooden bridge. It was a slow, steady climb. Most of the heavy work was getting up to the field. On top, the hill was as flat as an iron stove lid, perfect for growing hay.

"Farmer Parker talks to Sarge, Marty," Jerry said. "He calls, tells him what to do. Sarge seems to understand him."

"Good to know," Marty said.

"Are you going to the state fair?" Jerry asked.

"Yup."

"For fun, or are you showing?"

"I've got Sandy in a horse show, Friday."

"Schools let out Friday—fair day," Jerry said.

"He may be too young to win anything, but we'll see."

"Dick told me they're going to the girlie show," Jerry said.

"Him and Duba?"

"On the Midway. They're sneaking in under the show tent."

"I wouldn't put it past them," Marty said.

"They told me."

"Hope they're smart enough to leave their wallets in the car," Marty said.

"What's a Midway got to do with that?" Jerry asked.

"Midway is full of pickpockets come fair time and naked lady shows have a particular way of emptying a wallet, or so my gramps told me."

"Do girls really get—ya know—naked?"

"C'mon Sarge, keep a-going..." Marty grunted. "Well, I'm guessing they have a way of making you think they do, but I don't reckon the law would let 'em get naked," Marty said.

"Duba told me they get naked," Jerry said.

"They'd be arrested and hauled off. I think it's an illusion. I'm only guessing, mind you. I wouldn't know."

Marty slapped the reins down, gently but firm. The ride up the hill was a long, slow ride but steady. An empty wagon is an easy pull for a team of horses.

"I think we're going Friday."

"Look in the livestock show pavilion. Sandy and I'll be there for sure."

"Shaffer will be there with his rabbits," Jerry said.

"Never cottoned to rabbit," Marty said.

"You ever been on the Midway, Marty?"

"Well of course I've been on the Midway. Who hasn't?"

"Me and Holbrook, maybe some of the rest."

"But no, I've never been in the girlie show tent, if that's what you're driving at."

"I wasn't suggesting…" Jerry started.

"Oh, I stood around and listened to the barker a time or two, but I'd sure enough get my butt tanned six weeks to Sunday if my old man ever found out I went in—and he has a way of finding out things."

Jerry watched two rabbits stop their chewing, sit up and wait as the wagon passed on by up the hill.

"What's a pickpocket look like, anyway?" Jerry asked.

"If they knew that, there wouldn't be none, now would there?" Marty replied.

"So where should a guy carry his money if not in his pocket?"

"I wouldn't worry about it. What'll you have in your pocket, a buck? Two, maybe?"

"I've got money," Jerry said.

"They'll be looking for bigger fish than you. They'll be looking for farmers with cash on 'em, looking to buy a bull or livestock, maybe a new tractor…"

At the top of the hill, the team pulled to a level spot just before the gate. Jerry jumped off and pulled the gate back, so Sarge and Sally could get through and into the hayfield.

Five long rows of hay needed to be lifted into the wagon and taken down to the barn.

"Do you want Mayor and me to pull the hay-lift up to the back of the wagon so we can connect it?" Jerry asked.

"Way too heavy. I think I can line up straight enough and back into it," Marty said. "Sarge has done this plenty. Let's see if they can do it for me."

Mayor and Mary came over to watch.

"It might take us two trips, two full loads down," Marty said. "We'll see."

CHAPTER 5

DUCK AND COVER!

Marty reined the horses until they pulled around in a near half circle. He was lining them up with the first hay row on the field. He knew the horses would know what to do—keep the row of hay between them as they pulled. Barber climbed on and was now settin' alongside as lookout.

"Ktch, Ktch, let's go, Sarge!" Marty said. "Giddyap hosses, follow the hay line—like you know—follow the hay, Sarge."

The wheels rolled, metal hay lifter forks turned, screeched and scratched, spiking hay from the ground and carrying it up the lift a good ten feet before dropping it over the top and into the wagon. Mary and Jerry, standing in the back and waiting to spread the hay, kept their balance on the moving wagon leaning on their pitchforks.

"Spread it out," Marty shouted. "It'll dry faster."

Sarge and Sally picked up their gate.

It was haying time again on this field the horses knew so well. It was a walk in the park for them.

"Are you showing Sandy?" Barber asked.

"Plan to Friday," Marty said. "You showin' that ornery ring-nosed old bull of yours again?"

"Art and Bobby are," Barber said, "He's got blue ribbons. I'm thinking he's too old now. I'm going to have fun this year. Dick and Duba are driving us in on Friday."

"Did they offer, or were they trapped into it?"

"I think they were trapped, but Big Mike is giving us tickets to get in. He'll give you one, too, for helping the Parkers."

"They'll lose you, once you get there, I reckon," Marty said. "I heard they're up to no good."

"Why does the Midway have a reputation? Is it all that bad?" Barber asked.

"A state fair is about agriculture and industry; new cars and cooking, maybe. The side shows on a Midway are all about getting money from outta' your jean pockets into some huckster's pockets."

"Sounds like you've been there."

"I'm older than you guys; bound to have more experience. Let's say I've been around. Shucks, no harm walking the Midway, seeing the lights and sights. It's fun listening to it."

"You ever see the girls?"

"Girls?"

"You know—the 'woo-woo' girls."

"Oh, them. Some guy out front in a straw hat, waving a cane, would parade some fancies in sequins and garter straps and make a lot of promises, but no, I never went in."

"I wonder what it's like inside," Barber said.

"Wondering is just what the Midway is all about. The more they can get you to wonder, the more they can get you to pony up money to see if even half of what they say is true. Those Midway guys are slick."

Off in the distance Holbrook and Randy stepped through the gate and were walking the length of the field toward the wagon.

"Looks like the hay-fork lift is up and good to go," Marty said.

"T'ain't fair," Barber said. "I asked Pap about it—the Midway and all—he told me to tie my shoe, and run go fetch a bucket of water. And why wasn't I inside doing my homework?"

"Oh, I reckon it's a father's job to stall on some subjects. It's the mother's job to pray they never come up in the first place. Deny them if they do."

By this time there were only one and a half rows of the hay left on the field waiting to be picked up. The hay pile on the wagon was about seven feet high, with Mary and Jerry balancing on top.

"It's going to take two loads," Marty said.

Holbrook was standing about fifty feet directly in front, his back to the wagon looking north up into the sky.

"Hey, look!" He pointed. "Look, you guys!"

"What is that?" Tall Jerry shouted from atop the hay wagon.

"What's that?" Holbrook shouted, pointing off beyond the north side of the hill in front of them.

"Looks like an old biplane," Marty shouted. "Two wings, probably a relic '41, by the looks of it."

"Don't they give rides up at the state fair?" Mary shouted.

"Why's it wobbling all over like that," Holbrook shouted.

"I think it's in trouble," Barber said.

Off in the distance the plane broke through a high cloud, bringing it into better view. They could hear its single engine sputtering and popping. The horses acted up with the engine noises and the whine of the propeller.

"Easy, Sarge, easy Sally," Marty said, pulling on the reins, settling the team best he could. "Whoa there."

"It's coming right at us," Holbrook shouted.

"Oh, he's just putting on a show for his passenger, is all," Marty said. "Just showing off."

The plane came closer and closer, sputtering, poppin', wobblin' all get out—up and down, side and back headed right for the hill. That's when it started to dive.

"It's going to crash!" Jerry shouted. "Look! It's going down!"

"He's crashing!" Mayor shouted.

The plane dipped down out of sight, disappearing below the horizon on the north end of Parker's hill.

"It's crashing, it sure enough is," Marty snarled. "Get ready to go stomp a fire out. This whole field will go ablaze."

Marty no sooner got it out of his mouth when the plane swooped up and reappeared, roaring bigger than life over the horizon and barely clipping the edge of the hill with one wheel but snapping the top strand of barbed wire on the fence with the other, then bouncing back to earth and up off it again.

Blocking the sun, it was coming straight at the hay wagon now, the propeller blade whining like a fighter pilot, climbing again in front of Holbrook just enough to clear him and then the wagon.

Sarge and Sally reared up, kicking their hooves, whinnying, twisting their heads in fear.

"Jump! Duck for cover!" Marty shouted, pulling back on the reins.

"That pilot's crazy. He's going to kill somebody," Holbrook shouted.

"Easy, hoss, whoa there, boy. Easy, Sarge," Marty gruffed.

Getting the horses settled, Marty lay down on the seat bench, ducking his head, holding tight to the reins.

Those close by dropped low, scrambling under the hay wagon.

"Not under the wagon," Marty shouted. "If she rolls the hay lift will crush you. Stay away from the wagon wheels, too."

They edged from under the wagon and lay on the ground next to it, covering their heads.

The biplane sputtered up again toward the sky skippin' then poppin' a backfire. It circled the hayfield, turning up and down all over the place, wobbling like the pilot was trying to get someone's attention. Finally, it came down, bounced on its left wheel, jumped up off the ground then down on its right wheel before settling both wheels on the ground. It kept rolling along toward the end of the field, like the plane was on its own about to go through the fence and over the edge of the hill.

The pilot was alone in the plane in the back cockpit, his arm lifted, and a hand slapped at the steering stick swerving the plane around in a full circle. The slicing propeller kept idling, turning the plane, flashing the reflecting sun; the pilot's head slumped over. The plane rolled across the field every which way, like a serpentine.

"He's hurt," Marty barked.

"Maybe he's had a heart attack," Jerry said.

Everyone started running toward the rolling plane.

"Somebody try climbing on a wing, see if you can find a shut-off switch," Marty shouted. "Watch out for the propeller!"

"Be careful!" Mary said.

"Don't hit the stick," Mayor said. "That could turn it the wrong way."

"We have to shut it off. It could set the hayfield on fire," Marty shouted. "I've seen an Allis Chalmers' backfire send a barn up in smoke."

"It could crash through the fence and over the hill," Holbrook said. "We have to stop it."

Holbrook grabbed a stabilizing wire that held the upper and lower wings together. As the plane turned, he jumped on the back of the lower wing, pulling himself up using the wire. He climbed into the front cockpit and leaned over into the back cockpit where the pilot was. He bent his elbow over, locking it to the rear cockpit. The pilot's head was leaning back, his eyes closed under his goggles. Holbrook felt around with his hands, found knobs and switches and tried each, hoping to turn the engine off. He'd reach and click. With one, the plane rattled to a full stop, the propeller shaking before going silent and slowly becoming still.

"Mayor," Marty said, "grab the reins on Sarge and Sally and hold them steady! Don't let them spook. The rest of you help here. Let's get this guy out and onto the ground."

"The wing is canvas with lacquer on it, don't be stepping through it," Holbrook said.

Holbrook and Jerry were on one side of the cockpit, Marty and Randy on the other.

"Take his earphones and helmet off," Marty said. He pulled the goggles from the pilot and dropped them on the floor of the plane.

Mary was running to the gate of the field where they left the bucket of drinking water and ladle. Holbrook leaned in to unfasten the pilot's safety harness. As he did, the pilot started, opened his eyes and sat up.

"Where am I?" he grumbled.

Holbrook and Jerry bolted. They stood erect, eyes wide.

"Calm down, mister. You're in the hamlet called Delphi," blurted Marty. "You dang near crash-landed, but you're okay."

"Doesn't look like a hamlet," the man moaned. "Where's the hamlet?"

"We're up on a hill next to it. The hamlet is over there," Jerry said, pointing to the north edge of the field.

Randy pointed over the pilot's shoulder.

"Over there is the Delphi Falls. You're lucky you didn't crash into that."

The pilot opened his eyes, rolled them, turning his head about in a daze.

"I don't see any falls. Where's the falls? I don't see no hamlet, no houses. I don't see no falls."

"I'm no doc," Marty said, "but my dad would say he's delusional. I think he's in shock."

"Give him water," Mary said.

"Quick, help me get him out of this contraption and onto the ground," Marty said.

"Hey kid, I take objective to your insinulation. I am not diluse... dilo...what you said."

"Hang on, mister," Marty snapped.

"And this ish not a contraption. It's a fine piece of machinery."

"We'll discuss it all when we get you out and safe on the ground," Marty said. "Take his shoulder strap off."

Marty looked over at Holbrook and Jerry.

"In the state he's in, what would he know about shock?" Marty asked. "He's obviously in it. Just relax, fella. We'll get you out."

44

"That's shocking," the pilot squawked. "I heard that. What you said. I am def…defin…definitely not in shocked."

"Then what would you call it," Marty asked, trying to amuse the pilot, while putting the man's arm over his shoulder to help Randy lift him up and out of the cockpit.

Jerry and Holbrook grabbed his feet and lifted.

"You were either running out of gas, having fainting spells, or something that didn't look right, is all we know," Mayor said.

"We watched you nearly hit us," Holbrook said.

"It could have been a heart attack," Marty said. "What would you call that, mister?"

"I'd call it drunk," the pilot said.

They paused and stared at the pilot.

"I'm drunk," the pilot said.

"I think I can smell bourbon," Holbrook said. "I know what bourbon smells like."

"It's rye," the pilot said.

"Here's two empty bottles of something behind the pilot seat," Randy said.

Marty turned his head toward the man's face and sniffed at the air.

"Why, you're gassed!" Marty snorted. "This man is as drunk as a hard cider skunk."

"Where're the falls?" the pilot mumbled, as they rested him on the ground. "I don't see no falls."

The pilot plopped his head back, closed his eyes and passed out as Mary walked up with the bucket of water.

"Is he dead?" she asked.

"Dead drunk, is more like it," Marty said.

Mary knelt, loosened his tie and unbuttoned his collar.

CHAPTER 6

FRENCH, MAIS OUI. VICHY FRENCH, MAIS NON!

"Bring him in and set him on the couch," Farmer Parker said.

"Fay, you get back in bed," Mrs. Parker said.

Holbrook, Marty, and Mary helped the pilot to the couch, resting him back on it. Farmer Parker felt the man's pockets for guns or knives. Mrs. Parker put a pillow under his head and covered him with a blanket.

"Only two reasons a body will drink that serious," Farmer Parker said.

"These are children, Fay, careful what you say," Mrs. Parker said.

"He's a no-account or troublin'," Farmer Parker said.

"Yes, I agree," Mrs. Parker said.

"Or there's a woman," Farmer Parker said.

"Fay, get in bed," Mrs. Parker said.

"Let him sleep it off," Famer Parker said. "We'll know soon enough which way the wind blows for him."

"I can't imagine owning an airplane he'd be a no-account, Fay," Mrs. Parker said.

"Unless he stole it," Farmer Parker said.

"Let's go back up the hill," Marty said.

"I'm feeling good," Farmer Parker said. "I can help."

"You may think you're feeling good, Fay Parker," Mrs. Parker barked. "Dr. Brudny says one more day of rest and liniment. Get back in that bed, and you'll not be leaving me alone with a stranger in the house. What are you thinking?"

"Marty says we should have the hay in the loft by midday, and then we'll bury Buddy," Tall Jerry said.

"Who's tending the hay wagon?" Farmer Parker asked.

"Mayor and Barber are holding the reins until we get up there. Everything's fine," Marty said.

"How'd you get this man off the hill?" Farmer Parker asked.

"Sandy hefted him down on his back. Being deadweight, we could walk him down the hill like a pack mule."

It wasn't long before they were back up on the hayfield ready to go to work again.

"What'd you do with him?" Barber asked, as Marty and the rest walked toward the hay wagon.

"Parker took him in until we can see if he's okay," Holbrook said.

Mayor jumped off the wagon.

"They think he stole the plane," Barber said.

"Stop with that talk," Mary said. "No one thinks that. We think he's troubled maybe is all."

"Well I was just…" Barber started.

"Don't you have something to do, Barber?" Mary grunted as Barber turned and walked to the wagon.

"We were thinking of taking her around the last row and a half of hay," Mayor said. "But we figured sure enough if we did, something would break or bust."

"Well, let's get her loaded and down to the barn," Marty said. "When he wakes up, we'll see how he plans to get his plane off this hill."

The hay was loaded, fork-lifted and dropped into the barn hay mow. Marty unhitched and walked the horses out back, setting them loose in the pasture with a bucket of oats each. He whacked a gentle pat on their necks in thanks for getting through the day.

For Buddy's funeral, they lined up on the driveway for starters. Mrs. Parker stood on the back porch and watched. Farmer Parker managed to climb the pasture hill following behind Mary while the lads carried the dog in a gunny sack. Holbrook was carrying the shovel and they searched for sunny spots. When they settled on one, they rested the sack on the ground. Jerry untied the string, reached in and removed Buddy's collar, handing it up to Farmer Parker. Out of regard everyone stood in silence while Farmer Parker ran his fingers back and forth against the collar. Holbrook dug a grave, cleaned it square and nice, respectful-like. Jerry lowered Buddy down and each of them covered him with handfuls of dirt. Farmer Parker got on one knee and patted the dirt. He rested the stone in the middle of the grave. He whispered to Buddy that he put it there to keep cows from stepping on the grave.

"I've had some dogs in my lifetime," Farmer Parker said. "Never had words, ever I lost one. I'm not so good with words. I suppose wanting to say something says it well enough for me. Goodbye, old friend. I'll never be able to replace you…and I'm too old to try."

On the way down, Farmer Parker offered to help call the cows in come milking time that afternoon. The club wouldn't hear of it.

They didn't want to risk the wrath of Mrs. Parker for obliging the old man and getting him out of his sick bed any longer than a burial.

"We'll get the chores and the night milking done and come see you," Tall Jerry said.

"Supper's here tonight," Farmer Parker said. "Missus and Big Mike are stopping by with corn and roasted acorn squash."

"Can you fit us?" Barber asked.

"If you carry the picnic table from the back lawn and set her on the porch— that and bring out the kitchen table. Perfect day for eating out, not a black fly in the air," Farmer Parker said.

"Buddy can look down over us from the hill," Mary said.

In the barn, Holbrook turned the radio on for the milking and crawled up the wall ladder to throw down more hay. Jerry walked over to the ledge where Buddy used to sleep. He set the water bucket and ladle on the ledge to cause a body to think a good thought about the dog whenever they took a sip of water on the day of his burial.

All finished and hands rinsed with the hose, faces splashed, they let the cows out of the barn and led them up the drive, across the road and up Buddy's hill and pasture. That left them an hour before supper would be ready.

Mrs. Parker and Missus were organizing vittles in the kitchen. Most was settin' around the back porch recounting the day. Ole Charlie here was up on a side rail listening to ever' word and taking in the setting sun.

Farmer Parker and Big Mike were in a corner watching the young'uns growing up—wondering where the time had flown— when the pilot leaned a shoulder to push open the screen door, catching it with his hand and not letting it slam closed. He stepped out, running fingers through his hair and straightening his tie, wondering how hay got in his hair. He stepped out into the blinding setting sun and squinted.

"You nearly killed yourself," Marty said.

50

Marty was a reporter for the school newspaper. He didn't like mincing words. "What do you have to say for yourself?"

"That's enough, Marty," Mary said.

The pilot avoided looking into the lad's eyes. He looked instead over at Farmer Parker.

Marty was relentless.

"No, it isn't. He nearly killed us, too!"

The pilot rubbed his eyes, trying to wake up. He looked over at Farmer Parker again.

"You have a bottle?"

"We don't use it, son," Farmer Parker said.

"What were you thinking?" Marty snorted.

"There's one in the plane. Where's my plane?"

"The bottles in the plane are empty," Holbrook said.

"What were you thinking?" Marty repeated.

The pilot slumped in his chair, relenting.

"I wasn't trying to think," he mumbled, just to shut Marty up.

"What's that supposed to mean?" Marty asked.

"The plane was doing my thinking."

"Why that'd be suicide talk," Randy said.

"And that'd be *my* business now, wouldn't it?"

"Not if you killed us and a team of workhorses, it wouldn't," Marty barked. "That would be homicide."

"I 'spect you're right," the pilot said. "Sorry."

"Son," Farmer Parker said. "What could make a man in his prime want to give it all up like that? It doesn't make any sense."

Farmer Parker looked over at Big Mike. "What am I missing, Big Mike?"

"You seem like a good sort," Mrs. Parker said through the screen door.

"I know you have someone who cares for you," Missus said. "Your shirt is starched and creased with an iron."

"What could be so bad to make you want to kill yourself?" Mary asked.

"I'd already died, my friend. What's left to lose?" the pilot replied.

"You'd died? You're making no sense," Farmer Parker said. He turned to Big Mike again. "What does he mean?"

Big Mike thought it best to let the pilot speak for himself.

The pilot looked around the porch, trying to see a familiar face in all the eyes staring back at him.

"June 6, 1944 was the day I died. We climbed into the bellies of unheated airplanes in the pitch dark of night."

The pilot looked around at blank faces. "They dropped us from seven hundred feet up behind enemy lines on the Cherbourg peninsula—decoys for the boys landing on Omaha Beach."

The pilot paused.

He looked over at Farmer Parker.

"Was it horrible?" Mary asked.

"Ever see a dozen eggs?"

"Yes, of course."

"Crack a few of them. Adds up. Do that math on the five, six thousand dropped over Cherbourg alone getting shot at all the way down."

"How old were you when you jumped on D-Day?" Mayor asked.

"Seventeen."

"My God," Mrs. Parker said from behind the screen door.

Big Mike and Farmer Parker pursed their lips.

We had to jump—for France.

"How'd you get out?" Randy asked.

"A French farmer and his wife took me and two other jumpers in. They drew a map to Cherbourg so we could make it and not get captured."

"That was lucky," Barber said. "The French were loving to see you guys, I bet."

"Some were," the pilot said.

"What do you mean *some were*?" Mary asked. "France was our friend in the war."

"What's your name?"

"Mary."

"Well, Mary, there were the occupied French, and, yes, they were friendly 'allies,' but then there were the Vichy. They were French, too. Vichy was all high and mighty French, friendly with Hitler. Half of France stayed unoccupied by Hitler, left alone. French people

53

are good, hardworking—nice, decent folks—the Vichy French were bastards—helping Hitler, killing Jews."

Big Mike interrupted. "Let's give our guest some nourishment. Plenty of food here. Grab some salad and a plate."

Missus and Mrs. Parker came out with platters of food.

"What's your name, son?"

"Name's Ed, sir. Most call me Eddie."

"Well, Eddie," Big Mike said, "Eat hearty and rest up. You'll have tomorrow to figure how to get your plane off the hill. You're going to need your strength."

"Any chance a man can work his keep a day or so to earn gas enough to make it to Binghamton?"

"If'n a body's sober, there is," Farmer Parker said.

"How do you get your plane off the hill?" Randy asked.

"I'll fly it. Which hill is it on?"

"What's an old biplane like that need to take off, ya know, runway length?" Marty asked.

"Five hundred feet ought to do it."

"Well, hate to be the one to tell you, but I drove a wagon on it all day and it's at best three, four-hundred feet long with barbed wire fencing clear around it."

Eddie's shoulders slumped.

"Pass Eddie the corn," Big Mike said. "A night's sleep clears the head. You'll think better tomorrow."

"Eddie, you sleep on the couch tonight. Tomorrow, bunk in the barn," Farmer Parker said. "I'll come up with a chore or two."

CHAPTER 7

MARTY OPENS A CAN OF WORMS

Farmer Parker was settin' in the kitchen sipping coffee while Tall Jerry and his friends were on the back porch, yawnin' and stretchin' in the dark before going down to the barn to milk. He stepped outside to join them.

"Don't know how to thank you," Farmer Parker said.

"Why you're a full-fledged member of the Pompey Hollow Book Club, Farmer Parker. You would have done it for any of our families," Mary said.

"Dot dot dot—dash dash dash—dot dot dot," said Farmer Parker with a grin.

"You're an honored member," Randy said.

"How about we do a hayride as our thank-you? Sarge and Sally are up to a hayride."

"We could do it at our place," Barber said. "Mary, you could have your square-dance party then."

"Too cold for a hayride," Holbrook said.

"We can make it a regular hoedown," Mary said.

"Count us in," Farmer Parker said.

"Eddie can meet Hal, Bobby's dad," Barber said.

"Let me call Mrs. Barber and see if Wednesday will work for her," Mrs. Parker said. "It's a church night, but it may work."

"Eleven bells today will be the end of my days cooped up. Boss lady says I can take over my farm then. I get my reprieve."

"What about Eddie?" Holbrook asked.

"When he wakes, I'm going to let him whitewash the milking area in the barn. It needs a good going over."

"That was so sad," Mary said. "All of them dying like that, in another country."

Randy stepped in the house and picked the wall phone earpiece off the cradle and wound the crank.

"Myrtie, can you get my mom?" he asked.

"I don't recognize the voice."

"It's, Randy."

"Hello?"

"Mom, can Dad pick us up around eleven? We need rides."

Some scratchin' on the phone wire.

"What?"

Randy stuck a finger in his other ear.

"Speak up, Mom. I can hardly make you out."

"Where will you be?"

"We're still at Farmer Parkers."

"Your dad left on his milk-can route. He should be by soon."

"Oh, okay. But if we miss him will you tell him?"

"I will."

"Thanks, Mom."

Click.

Randy stepped outside. "She said my dad will be here to pick up Parker's milk cans. We can tell him ourselves."

Mary, Tall Jerry, and the gang were near the barn when they noticed a small, bright light up top of the hayfield hill.

"What's that?" Tall Jerry asked.

"Looks like it's moving," Barber said.

"Somebody's coming down the hill," Holbrook said.

"They're carrying a lantern," Jerry said.

"You guys wait here," Mary said. "Let us know."

Holbrook and Jerry walked toward the back gate. Barber, Mayor, Randy, and Mary went into the barn.

About the time the glow made it to the wooden bridge, the clunking sounds of hooves gave it away.

Through the fog they could make out Marty riding Sandy up the knoll to the gate. Marty was holding the lantern out to the side.

"We thought you went home last night," Jerry said.

"I slept in the barn."

"What for?" Jerry asked.

"I left for home but started thinking and turned around at Doc Webb's place and came back."

"What were you thinking?" Jerry asked.

"I wanted to see if I could find some clues. I needed to take a good look at the airplane again."

"Did you find any clues?" Holbrook asked.

"I found this," Marty said.

He handed a leather satchel valise down to Jerry.

"Give it to Eddie when he wakes up," Marty said.

"Did you open it?" Holbrook asked.

"Naw," Marty said. "Didn't have to. Pretty much got all the clues I needed looking in the plane."

"Like what, for example?" Jerry asked.

"What kind of clues?" Holbrook asked.

"I found a crumpled sack he carried whiskey in. There was a handwritten receipt in it. He got two bottles at the same time, yesterday. He must have emptied one and thrown it out while he was flying."

"Why's that a clue?" Holbrook asked.

"The one in the plane was empty too," Marty said.

"We know he was drunk," Holbrook said.

"What else, Marty?" Jerry asked.

"The gas tank was on empty," Marty said. "I tapped on it to see if the needle was broken."

"What does it all mean?" Holbrook asked.

Marty handed the lantern to Jerry, stepped down off Sandy and began removing the bridle and saddle.

"It means Eddie has some explaining to do. He's not telling us everything. I want to ask him some questions. He may be in trouble he's not telling us about. He may need help."

"What makes you think that?" Jerry asked. "Anybody can get drunk once in a while. Doesn't make him suspicious."

"A man empties two pints of rye flying a plane eighteen miles on a near empty tank of fuel? He might as well have been holding a gun to his head. Only two possible answers."

Marty was smart. Jerry and Holbrook were all ears.

"He was so despondent he was thinking suicide like he was talking last night."

"Or?" Holbrook asked.

"Or he had so much on his mind he wasn't thinking straight before his takeoff," Marty said.

"Which do you think?" Jerry asked.

"Maybe both," Marty said. "Let's see what he has to say for himself."

Randy was pouring milk through the strainer when Eddie came in. Looking sheepish, he tried to avoid eye contact as he checked for a whitewash bucket and brush. Marty reached up and turned the radio volume down. Holbrook walked over and handed Eddie his valise.

"I thought I lost this," Eddie said.

"It was in your plane," Holbrook said.

"Thanks."

Eddie unzipped the top of the valise, widening the mouth of it.

"It's all there," Marty said. "We didn't open it."

"I wasn't worried," Eddie said. "Just forgot what I had in it."

Eddie pulled a handbill and ten printed tickets, fanned them in his hand and offered them.

"Like Sherlock Holmes, anybody? I got ten tickets to the Sherlock Holmes Players. They'll be up in New Woodstock Sunday—matinee and evening show. Good for passage into either show. Want 'em, anybody? Free if you want them."

"Eddie," Marty said.

"You want them, Marty?"

"You've been dancing about, bobbing and weaving," Marty said. "Truth of the matter is you about killed us and you at least owe us what's eating you, so we can get it behind us."

"We might even be able to help," Randy said.

"No offense, but how can a bunch of schoolkids help?"

"What?!" Holbrook barked.

"What could you know about life, anyway?"

Mary pushed Holbrook aside and stepped around Randy to get up near enough to Eddie's nose to get his full attention. He was taller, but she was about to bring him down to size.

"Listen buster," she began. "Who do you think you are feeling sorry for yourself like you put on? You were scared and had to jump out of an airplane—big deal. My daddy's ship was torpedoed. Half the kids we know lost somebody in the war. Little Bobby's mom was killed by a bomb, and she was a nurse. We were all scared. Being scared doesn't give you any right to be rude."

"I'm sorry…" he started.

"Sorry nothing," Mary blurted. "We dumb schoolkids who don't know life have caught burglars; we've chased off POWs; and us hick kids have run a farm for an old man who hurt himself on a ladder. You owe us more than *'sorries'* buster."

"But…" Eddie started.

"You want our help, you'd better start fessin' up," Marty said.

Mary stepped back, taking a deep breath.

Her friends stood around, their mouths open.

"Yeah!" Mayor snorted, adding a knockout blow.

"And I'll take those Shakespeare tickets," Randy said.

"Sherlock Holmes," Marty said.

"Whatever," Randy snapped. "I'll take those, too."

Eddie turned a beet red, looked Mary in the eye, handing Randy the tickets. He stepped across the gutter, picked up the milking stool Barber was finished with and squatted on it.

"I'm a house painter. Most of the year I make a living painting houses and stores for folks in Binghamton. I'm married to the same woman since 1946, and we have two girls."

Mary, Holbrook, Mayor and Tall Jerry sat on the barn floor cross-legged. Randy and Barber were arranging the milk cans but listening. Marty raised an arm and leaned on a cow.

"Painting isn't so good in winter. Every year about this time, I get a chance to earn extra money."

"Airplane rides at the state fair?" Marty asked.

"Yep," Eddie said.

"Figured," Marty said.

"It goes pretty good at the fair. I usually bring in enough money to get us through if the weather holds good for flying."

"Did your airplane break down?" Mary asked.

"No."

"Did it rain in Syracuse?" Barber asked.

"It was my best year ever. I had six hundred forty dollars yesterday morning—enough to have some left for Christmas for the girls."

"What happened?" Marty asked.

"Packing to leave, I chocked the plane where I always do and put a couple bucks in my shirt pocket like I always do. I try to win kewpie dolls for my girls before I gas up and head home. I had good money from the week and a painting job waiting on me back in Binghamton…"

"And?" Marty asked.

"And a guy came up offering me these tickets free. Said they were trying to 'paper' the house, he called it and held them out for the taking. Paper the house—that means they give away tickets, so the play looks successful and seats are full."

"And?" Marty asked.

"He had a French accent, so I asked him where he was from. I'm thinking he might know the farmer who hid me out in '44. He said *Moulins*. I kept a straight face, mind you, never flinched. I just told him I was leaving town and couldn't use his tickets and started to walk away."

"Why didn't you want the tickets?" Randy asked.

"He was going home, he couldn't use them," Holbrook said.

"He maybe could have traded them for chances at kewpie dolls," Marty said. "Why'd you walk away from the guy, Eddie?"

"Know where Moulins is?"

"No," Mary said. "Tell us."

"Moulins is in Vichy," Eddie snarled.

"The bad French guys," Holbrook said.

"Nazis in French uniforms," Eddie said.

"Let me guess," Marty said. "He insisted you keep the ten tickets, even slipped them in your valise, all friendly and polite."

"Yep," Eddie said.

"Only thing was he was a pickpocket and lifted your money out of the valise without you seeing it at the same time he put the tickets in."

"I need a drink," Eddie said.

"No drinking," Mary growled.

"What's your name?" Eddie asked.

"Marty."

"Marty's right. That's what happened."

"That does it! Tall Jerry, we need Dick. We're calling an SOS. Barber, figure how to get word to Dick and Duba."

"They're in school today," Barber said.

"Figure it out!" Mary said.

"Let's get the cows back to pasture," Jerry said. "Mayor, you and Marty hitch Sarge and Sally and haul the spreader to the hayfield and spread it. Then put the horses to pasture."

"We meet in the cemetery…" Mary started. "What time is it?"

"Seven thirty a.m.," Eddie said looking at his watch. "Easy you don't get too close with the spreader and hit my plane with that stuff."

"We'll all meet up at ten," Mary said.

She turned to Eddie. "Don't just sit there," she said. "Whitewash the milk room. It's not all that big. Get it done and be ready to go with us."

"Where to?"

"To our meeting at the Delphi cemetery," Mary said.

"For what?" Eddie asked.

"The Pompey Hollow Book Club is about to get your money back for you. Best you put a move on and make that milk room pretty for Farmer Parker to inspect before we go."

They saw a lantern coming down the hill

CHAPTER 8

GETTING IT ALL OUT ON THE TABLE

They were making plans to head on to the cemetery meeting when Big Mike drove down around the hill. A farmer's morning started around five o'clock. A baker starts loading bread trucks with warm bread around two in the morning. He was coming from the bakery for his early morning nap before going back to work. He caught their eye and pulled in Farmer Parker's drive.

"Mum's the word," Tall Jerry said.

"Cheese it," Mary warned out of the side of her mouth.

"Ribs and corn tonight," Big Mike said. "We'll see you get rides home."

Big Mike saw Eddie coming out of the barn.

"Any thoughts about the plane, Eddie?"

With the new developments of state fair pickpocket intrigue, they forgot about helping Eddie get his biplane off the hill. That was a priority, so he could get home.

"Stepped out to get some air," Eddie said. "Whitewashing the milk-can room and racks. I haven't had a chance to think about my plane. Later this morning, I will."

Eddie looked across the Cardner Road bridge on Big Mike's side of the road, next to the alfalfa field.

"Over there," he said, pointing. "Anybody know who owns it? I could take off from that field. It looks long enough," Eddie said.

"No one will mind the plane using the field for take-off," Big Mike said.

"All right to park it there while I earn travel money?" Eddie asked.

"I'll see who owns it and get their okay, but I'm sure there won't be a problem," Big Mike said.

"Thank you," Eddie said.

"Have any idea how you'll get it down off the hill?" Big Mike asked.

"How about on the hay wagon," Mary asked. She puffed a curl from her eye.

"Plane's too heavy," Big Mike said. "The wagon's wheels can't hold that weight."

He turned and walked toward his car. He turned again.

"Tell you what. After my nap, on my way back to the bakery, I'll stop at Conway's and ask if Jimmy could bring their tractor over after school. That tractor might do the job."

"Conway is Minneapolis Moline Conway to us," Holbrook said.

"His tractor is enormous," Mary said.

"He'll get it down the hill," Mayor said.

"The biggest tractor in the Crown. We've seen it lift a car," Tall Jerry said.

"It has a front-end lift thing-a-ma-jiggy," Mary said.

It was settled.

Farmer Parker, hearing the tail-end of the conversation, came out.

"Eddie, I'll fill the plane with gasoline plus some money for your whitewashing," Farmer Parker said.

"I'm hosing the floor down," Eddie said. "I'm touching up beams and the radio shelf with whitewash. Might as well hit it all so long as there's enough whitewash left after the parlor is done. I got time."

"That'll be fine, son," Farmer Parker said. "I'll kick in another few bucks for your trouble."

Mrs. Parker handed Mary a sack with sandwiches and farm butter pickles wrapped in wax paper.

"The butter pickles are my secret recipe," Mrs. Parker said.

"Can I sleep in the barn until I get my plane off the hill and am able to take off?"

"Help yourself, son," Farmer Parker said. "Use the straw loft. You can earn keep and food helping around the place until you leave. The chicken coop needs repair. Hammer and nails in the shed. There's an old toolbox in there somewhere."

Marty nudged Jerry in the ribs.

"Ask him," he whispered.

"Huh?" Jerry grunted.

"Ask him to tell Dick about meeting us," Marty whispered. "Go on, ask him."

"Dad," Tall Jerry said. "When Dick gets home can you tell him we're meeting at the cemetery, and we need him and the older guys?"

There was nothing could put a grin on Big Mike's face more than an adventure. He winked at Jerry and walked to his car.

Tall Jerry turned the farm over in good repair, cows milked, hay in, manure spread, and chores done. Farmer Parker accepted it with a tip of his hat and a handshake.

Mary twisted the lunch sack closed. Side-by-side they headed down over the wooden bridge and up the hill. At the top they circled around the biplane, like it was an exhibit in a museum. They listened to Eddie about learning to fly when he was fourteen; his doing backward loops and barrel rolls; banking around silos and getting yelled at by farmers for scaring cows. He told of his flying above a freight train in Pennsylvania and busting through the smoke from its coal engine stack just before climbing straight up in the sky and missing the tunnel and mountainside. Of how quiet it was looking down at snow-capped mountains in the Adirondacks under a full moon.

Mary passed around sandwiches and butter pickles.

"How high will she go?" Mayor asked.

"Couple of miles—maybe could push her up to ten thousand feet. Top speed is right at 106 miles per hour," Eddie said.

Holbrook grabbed the tail of the plane with two hands and gently lifted it off the ground.

"Look, we can lift it onto the hay wagon," Holbrook said. "It's not heavy. We could carry it down."

"That's the tail," Eddie said. "The front end weighs a ton or more."

"We have to be careful we don't rip a wing," Mayor said.

"Hitting a tree branch or fence posts," Mary said.

"Dropping it could hurt the propeller," Tall Jerry said.

"That would put me out of business," Eddie said.

"What are your girl's names?" Mary asked.

"Judy and Lucy."

"That's sweet."

"Cute as buttons."

"Have you telephoned them?" Mary asked.

Eddie didn't answer.

"Your wife, too. They're probably worried."

Eddie tipped his head, shrugged his shoulders in a 'maybe' sign, avoiding the subject, and stepped to the plane. He lifted a side panel and pulled a dipstick to check the oil.

Mary could see he was edgy with the position he found himself in, losing the money, nearly killing himself—having to explain a lot to his wife and family. She walked over.

"We can get your plane down off the hill."

"You think so?"

"There's more, but you have to listen and not walk away."

"I'm listening," Eddie said. "Don't you guys think I'm not appreciative."

"We maybe can get your money back."

"Sure you can. A bunch of kids."

"You say that again, Eddie, and I swear I'll sock you in the nose."

"Sorry."

"And stop apologizing."

"Sorry."

"We have the Pompey Hollow Book Club. These guys are most of the regulars, but other kids join up all the time."

"A book club is going to get my money back? I don't think so."

"Barber only came up with that name so we could get out of the house for meetings when we were nine and ten."

Eddie grinned.

"We've caught crooks before, and we caught two POWs who escaped Pine Camp. The Army gave our towns ambulances because of us."

"I believe you," Eddie said.

"So, here's the deal," Mary said. "It's not just about your plane anymore. It's about your family. It's about letting us figure a way to get your money back. We've called an SOS."

"An SOS?"

"That's when the older guys help us—like get your plane down and get your money back," Mary said.

"If they only could," Eddie said.

"Just wait. They're good."

"What do you want me to do?"

"Come to the cemetery and listen," Mary said.

Walkin' abreast, Marty on one end and Mary and Eddie on the other, the gang strolled from the biplane, crossing the hayfield and climbing the back hill down into the cemetery. As they gathered around ole Charlie's headstone, cars pulled in, crunching up the cinder drive. Dick in his Willys coupe, Duba driving his pickup, and Conway in his new Chevrolet, with Jimmy Dwyer sitting alongside. They got out and strutted all important-like, looking like the James gang.

"What's up?" Dick barked.

"Spill," Duba sparked.

"How'd you guys get here so fast?" Mary asked.

"Big Mike told Principal it was an emergency," Conway said.

"Principal called us to his office and let us leave," Duba said.

"We figured you'd be here," Conway said.

"What's up?" Dick asked.

"Spill it," Duba repeated.

Mary puffed a curl from her eye and looked at her watch. It was past 1:00 p.m.

"Sit down, this might take a while."

"We've got all day," Dick said, lighting two cigarettes with his last match and handing one to Duba.

"When I get through, we can decide if we call an SOS. If we do, we can meet some more before supper."

"Ribs and corn," Holbrook said.

Eddie was sitting on the grass.

"Eddie, SOS is what we call it when we think we need the older guys, because they can drive."

"You just start the club?" Eddie asked.

"We started in 1949. Most of us were nine or ten."

Eddie looked over at Dick and Duba. "You guys had licenses since 1949?"

"Nobody said anything about licenses," Dick said.

"Didn't you learn to fly at fourteen?" Mayor asked.

"I did," Eddie said.

"We learned to drive at twelve," Dick said.

"We could rebuild a six-cylinder engine at sixteen," Duba said.

"Okay, guys, Eddie here was robbed at the fair and we need to help him."

Mary wasted little time bringing the older guys up to snuff.

"Marty found some clues, so I think he should talk," Mary said. "Marty, you tell them about it."

"Not much to tell," Marty said. "Eddie here earned six hundred dollars or so giving plane rides at the state fair and got pickpocketed."

They get all of his six hundred dollars?" Dick asked.

"It was a little more, but yes, he got it all," Eddie said.

"Would you know his face?" Conway asked.

"I'd know his face, you bet I'd know his face," Eddie said.

"Eddie says he's a Vichy French crook handing out fliers for the Sherlock Holmes Players show for next Sunday," Marty said.

"What does that mean, Vichy French?" Duba asked.

"France was divided in two in the war," Dick said. "Allied France and our enemy, Vichy France."

"You know your history," Eddie said.

"Eddie's family depends on his state fair money to get through the winter," Mary said. "He lives in Binghamton."

"His plane's stuck on Parker's hill and it ain't long enough for a takeoff," Marty said.

"We need to get it down to the field next to our alfalfa field," Tall Jerry said.

"Eddie can take off on that," Mayor said.

Dick stood and stepped in front.

That was the signal. The older guys were taking on the SOS.

"Listen up," Duba barked, squatting down on one knee.

Mary stepped away and sat down.

"Synchronize your watches," Dick said. We meet back here at five-thirty—set your watches now at two."

"We're having another meeting tonight?" Holbrook asked.

"We'll go to supper at five-thirty, but we all leave together from here," Dick said.

He began organizing his thoughts and giving directives, as he had before they cornered the POWs on Halloween.

"Conway, you and Dwyer go get the Moline," Dick said.

"That's a tractor," Eddie said.

"Yes," Conway said.

"You can't drag the plane," Eddie said.

"The Moline isn't just a tractor, Eddie, it's a huge tractor," Jerry said. "It should be able to lift it."

"Haul the plane off the hill and down to the field," Duba said.

"Barber," Dick said. "You, Tall Jerry, Randy, Mary, Bases, and Holbrook go with them and help."

"Remember," Duba said. "Conway's boss up there."

"We'll remember," Mary said.

"If you have to pull out fence posts to get the plane through, go ahead and do it, but put them back better than before," Dick said.

"Fix all the wires if you cut wires," Duba said.

"The tractor should lift it up and over the fence," Conway said.

"That would be the best way," Duba said.

"Eddie, if there're keys to the plane, give them to Conway," Dick said. "Marty, you and Eddie come with us."

"Who's us?" Marty asked.

"Me, Eddie, and Duba," Dick said.

"Why me?" Marty asked.

"You know the fairgrounds better than anyone because of the horse shows. We'll need you at the library."

"School's not out for hours," Mary said.

"So?" Duba asked.

"How're you going to sneak Eddie into the school library?"

"Eddie," Dick said. "Didn't I hear that play was on Sunday?"

"Sherlock Holmes. Yes, it's playing two times on Sunday," Eddie said.

"Then we've got some serious homework to do and not much time if we're going to be ready. They'll all be gone after Sunday. Jump in the car, we'll head to the Cazenovia Public Library," Dick said.

"This will change everything," Mary said.

"What's changed?" Tall Jerry asked.

"It looks like we'll be meeting here the rest of the week," Holbrook said.

71

"Barber, find out if we can play my records and dance at your place Wednesday," Mary said.

"Barn dance, hayride?" Barber asked.

"It'll give Farmer Parker the chance of having a hayride," Mary said.

"Eddie, where's the play going to be?" Dick asked.

"New Woodstock, on Sunday," Eddie said.

"Are you sure the Sherlock Holmes Player thing is in New Woodstock and not in Cazenovia?" Duba asked.

"I'll check. It's printed on the flier that's in my valise," Eddie said. "I thought it was in New Woodstock."

"It's in New Woodstock," Randy said, holding up a ticket.

"If you get the plane off the hill, can you find a tarp somewhere and put it over the cockpit?" Eddie asked.

The group assured him as they dispersed. Dick, Duba, Eddie, and Marty heading to Cazenovia—by way of Farmer Parker's to pick up Eddie's valise. Mary and crew climbing the hill to the biplane, and Conway and Dwyer driving to get the Moline.

CHAPTER 9

DARKNESS AFFECTS US ALL

For the first time as a guardian angel, a fright was comin' over ole Charlie here today.

It's just that this here French Vichy pickpocket and the talk of State Fair girlie shows and Sherlock Holmes stage performers from across the water are new to me and not settin' right in my gut.

I wasn't never afraid of things I knew about. I would know what I would be praying for. But here and now I was afraid of the unknown. Ole Charlie here needed educating in a world I wasn't accustomed to—and I needed it soon so I could deal with it all.

Might say this ole country farmer with nothing but half an acre and a two-room house, an outdoor privy and a small chicken coop when I was alive was now in water over my head.

Tonight's moon would be full, and a full moon is opportunity for an angel. I could pray for an Angel Congress on top of Big Mike's barn garage roof for later tonight. Angels can do that under a full moon—pray for help. I twinkled word into heaven I needed special help with my education about Paris show ladies-of-entertainment, Sherlock Holmes stage actors and about pickpocket scoundrels. Word came back to me to be on Big Mike's barn garage roof at ten o'clock. My prayers would be answered.

While I was praying for help here in Delphi Falls, up in Cazenovia, Dick and Duba were trying to get past the front desk at the Cazenovia Public Library.

"Young man, I need to see your library card," the bespectacled matron of the books said.

73

"But ma'am…" Dick started.

"No library card, no books."

"Ma'am, I don't have one, but we have important research to do," Dick said.

"I'm sorry. You need a library card."

"It could be a matter of life and death. Can't we just go into your reference section?" Duba asked.

"We promise to be quiet," Dick said.

"If it's life or death, what you need is a police station, not a library. You'll find Sheriff…"

"Ma'am, okay, I exaggerated about life and death, but this is important."

"You need a library card."

"Can he sign up now and get one?" Duba asked.

"Please keep your voices down."

"Well, can I?" Dick asked.

"Your parents would have to sign for you. Books are a responsibility. They are expensive. A parent would need to sign for you."

"I'm twenty-five. Could I get a library card?" Eddie asked.

The matron looked him over, unshaven.

"Where do you live?" she asked

"I'm day labor, staying at Farmer Parker's place down in Delphi Falls," Eddie said. "If you call, I'm sure they'll vouch for me."

"Is that in Cazenovia?" the matron asked.

"Our place, he stays at our place," Dick interrupted. "Delphi Falls. That's in Cazenovia."

"You boys go on in, but don't make noise, keep your voices down, and put all the books back where you found them. If you don't remember, don't guess. Bring them here for me to put away."

They moved quickly, with Dick giving simple direction.

"Eddie, pull out anything you can find—magazines, reference books, anything on World War II that talks about the Vichy French."

"Will do. Anything else?"

"Check and see if Hemingway wrote about the Vichy."

"I'll look in the index cards," Eddie said.

"Duba, find what you can on English acting companies and the Sherlock Holmes Players," Dick said. "Check through local newspapers for articles."

"Okay," Duba said.

"Marty, find a map of the fairgrounds in Syracuse."

In time Eddie carried a stack of LIFE magazines and *Saturday Evening Post* magazines from the early 1940s. He found two volumes of the Encyclopaedia Britannica with war pictures. He and Dick started to go through them all page by page, combing for clues.

"Look at this," Dick said. "I never knew this before. France was divided into two parts in the war. Here's a map."

France in WWII – Occupied and Vichy (free)

"It's just like you said, Eddie, one part of France, under General de Gaulle, was occupied by the Germans. The other part had a bad

75

French guy Marshal Philippe Petain, who was like ninety and left over from World War I. He ran the second part of France, in the south—Vichy."

Vichy French Marshal Philippe Petain shaking Hitler's hand.

"He was friends with Hitler. The Nazis left him alone."

"Any ideas?" Eddie asked.

"Not yet," Dick said.

"I'm not finding anything on the Sherlock Holmes Players," Duba said.

"Let's find the playhouse where they're performing Sunday and snoop around," Dick said.

"Seeing all this Vichy stuff is making me think," Eddie said.

"Good," Dick replied.

"Something's bothering me."

"Like what?"

"You know what's bothering me about this whole thing?"

"What?" Dick asked.

"I was there a long time, in England."

"So?"

"The Germans kept bombing England all throughout the war. The Blitz, they called it."

"What's that got to do with…?" Dick started.

"They killed a lot of people in England—kids and families."

"I know," Dick said. "They sent V-2 rockets day and night."

"They sent thousands of them. Sometimes they would bomb London using blimps. They called them dirigibles," Eddie said.

"So, what's your point?" Dick asked.

"The Vichy French helped Hitler all through the war, even while they were bombing England day and night," Eddie said.

"I know it was bad, Eddie. I just don't know where you're going with all this," Dick said.

"Think about it. Vichy French were enemies. They even arrested French citizens who were Jews and the Gypsies, even prostitutes—what they called 'undesirables.' They sent them to concentration camps to be killed or to work as slave labor."

Eddie opened a page in LIFE Magazine. "Take a look at these pictures," he said

This drawing shows how the Vichy made phony trucks out of canvas. They would hide under them to lure Gypsies, so they could capture them. Sometimes they hid cannons under them, like this one."

"You're trying to make a point," Dick said.

"Any Englishmen who lived through the Blitz bombings isn't ever going to forget what they did to the English," Eddie said. "Not in eight or ten years anyway they won't."

"I think I'm seeing where you're going," Dick said.

"I saw London after the War. It'll take years to rebuild it. The Vichy were the Nazis."

"And so?" Dick asked.

"No way would an English acting company hire a Vichy Frenchman with the Blitz still fresh in their memories. Maybe that pickpocket was only pretending to be Vichy French—trying not to leave a trail."

"Are you saying…?"

"I'm saying maybe he was pretending to be Vichy French."

"If we could only prove it," Dick said.

"Too bad we don't speak French," Duba said.

"Wait!" Dick said. "Say that again!"

"Say what?" Duba asked.

"What you just said."

"Too bad none of us speak French?"

"Hold tight," Dick barked.

He stood and walked over to Marty at another table.

"Found anything on the fairgrounds?"

"Some old photographs of it is all. Nothing like what you're looking for—a map of the grounds."

"That's okay, you can draw one best you can from memory," said Dick. "I have a new job we need to get done."

"Name it," Marty said.

"I need you to memorize these pictures of the Gypsy wagons and the one made of canvas—here, this one. Sketch that one on a piece of paper."

"And?" Marty asked.

"Get with Mrs. Coco, the art teacher—and Mr. Ossant in the school shop. We need a Gypsy wagon, maybe out of canvas."

"You mean you want a canvas tent that looks like a Gypsy wagon, with wheels but it's not a wagon, just a tent that looks like a wagon?" Marty asked.

"Yes."

"I'll need a ride to school," Marty said.

"We'll take you. Give us a second."

Dick stepped around the library tables leaning in and quietly asking people reading if they spoke French. A lady paging through a book looked up and smiled.

"Why yes," she said. "I speak and read French."

"Would you hold on for a minute, lady?" Dick asked.

Dick waved Eddie over and sat him down next to the lady.

"Lady, this is Eddie. He was a paratrooper who landed in France behind enemy lines on D-Day."

"Well, I've never been to France," the lady said, "but thank you for helping bring an end to that terrible war, young man."

"Eddie," Dick whispered, "this is important."

"What?" Eddie asked.

"You have to remember anything that French pickpocket said to you."

"You're kidding, right?" Eddie asked. "That happened days ago."

"You have to try," Dick said.

"Did he speak French?" the lady asked.

"He spoke English with a heavy French accent," Eddie said.

"What did he say?" Dick asked. "Try to remember."

"He said he was helping the actors paper the theater seats next Sunday so there would be filled seats in the audience," Eddie said.

"That doesn't make him French," Dick said.

"Oh, he was Vichy French all right. He even called me '*mon ami.*' He sounded like the French farmer who hid us in their barn."

"I'm not sure," Dick said.

"I even knew the town the pickpocket was from was Vichy French. He made a big deal that the bigger the crowd the better the wankers would act, and so the better his Sherlock Holmes show would be," Eddie said.

"The man isn't French," the lady said.

"Huh?" Dick bolted.

"He's British."

"Just from what he said you can tell?" Dick asked.

"He's a Brit. He's used a pejorative that is English, not French. A Frenchman would not have used the word."

"What's a pejorative?" Dick asked.

"A dirty word," Duba said.

"It's a local slang term—probably London or Liverpool—a schoolboy word. And not a nice one," the lady said.

"What word?" Dick asked. "Can you say it?"

"Wanker."

"Wanker?" Dick whispered.

"That is a 'naughty'— well, let's say an undesirable word," the lady said.

"You sure he said it, Eddie?"

"Positive."

"It's English slang used by the young from time to time. He's definitely English," the lady said.

Dick went into detail how Eddie was pickpocketed, and explained that the ruse was his trying to give away the Sherlock Holmes tickets.

"Aren't you the group that caught the POW escapees?" she asked.

"Guilty," Duba said.

"I want to help," she said. "How can I help?"

"I can't believe I got duped like that," Eddie said.

"The man was with the Sherlock Holmes Players. I'd bet on it," the lady said. "Maybe a stagehand, though. But he's careful. He didn't want to draw any suspicion on the players, so he pretended he was French."

"Vichy French," Duba said.

"He probably recognized your leather flight jacket," Dick said.

"He wanted to throw your memory off-guard," the lady said.

"Which he was able to do with the Vichy lie—at least for a while," Marty said.

"Exactly," the lady replied. "For all you knew he was hired to pass out tickets. He would never suspect you looking for him—a Vichy Frenchman—at the theater where Brits are playing."

"This Saturday," Duba said. "We'll give him a taste of his own medicine."

"Thanks for your help," Dick said.

"Best of luck," the lady replied.

As they walked out of the library toward Dick's car, Eddie asked, "What's next?"

"Let's see how they're getting along with the plane. Then we'll get supper. Later we'll finish coming up with a plan."

"And we'll attack the Vichy French." Eddie laughed.

"You've got that right," Dick said.

"I get it!" Duba said. "If the pickpocket believes Eddie was convinced he's Vichy French, the better our chances of getting the money back."

"And the more he believes we're Gypsies, rolling in gold and silver and dripping with expensive jewelry…" Dick said.

"Oh, wow!" Duba said.

"With a genuine Gypsy wagon," Marty said.

Eddie beamed a smile and climbed into the front seat of Dick's car.

"I think I'll telephone my wife tonight. See how the girls are—say hello," Eddie said.

CHAPTER 10

DOWN-TO-EARTH PHYSICS

The engineering a body could learn living on a farm and having to think up solutions is amazing. War younglings learned early that anything could be done if they put a mind to it and worked together. A biplane stuck on top of the hill needed to come down. Conway got his tractor up there, but after measuring off what parts he had on the tractor that might be of service and stepping-off measuring the plane, he concluded something had to give.

"Oh, she'll lift it off the ground all right," Conway said. "But I don't like the tilt we'd have riding it down the hill. It could tip us over."

"Pretty steep," Holbrook said.

Holbrook, Randy, and Mayor had removed two gate fence posts in preparation.

About this time Dick, Duba, Eddie, and Marty made their way to the top of the hill and were walking toward the biplane. Dick gestured to keep quiet, letting the ones at it do their jobs.

"Let's sit and watch," he whispered.

He knew every person there. They were all smart as whips and would figure it out. The four squatted on the ground thirty feet away from the plane.

"I got an idea," Mary said.

Conway turned the tractor engine off.

"Let's hear it."

"The plane, with its crazy shape and different weight all around is hard to balance."

"That's it in a nutshell," Conway said.

"It could tip over," Holbrook said.

"And it being canvas covered, it's fragile in certain parts, making it harder to get hold of," Mary said.

"We might rip a wing or tear the canvas with a wrong move," Conway said.

"What if we took it down the hill level, not tilted?" she asked. "Would that do it?"

"No offense, Mary," Conway said. "A hill goes up and down, there ain't nothing level about a hill, either way you're headed."

"Well, if it was level," Mary said. "I mean what if we could make it level?"

"Then we'd be down there at the bottom and not up here on top," Conway said impatiently.

"It's not impossible," Mary said.

"Impossible!" Conway barked.

"You're not listening," Mary said.

"Even forgetting the hill, the plane doesn't have anything level enough on it to lift it off the ground level. We can't take the propeller off. We can't put it upside down, nose first on the forklift," Conway said.

"But the tractor could lift the hay wagon level, couldn't it?" Mary asked.

"You seem to forget, Mary, we're lifting an airplane," Conway said.

"No need to get snippy, Conway. Could the tractor lift the hay wagon level?" Mary asked.

"Yes, but I don't get your point. We're not lifting a hay wagon."

"We could bring the hay wagon up here," Mary said.

"We've gone over all that, Mary. The wagon won't hold the weight of the plane," Conway said.

"The wheels," Mary said.

"Huh?" Conway asked.

83

"Big Mike said the wheels wouldn't support the plane?"

"Yup!"

"What if we take the wheels off, setting it flat on the ground? We roll the plane onto the wagon on the ground and strap it down. The Moline could lift the flat hay wagon, plane and all—and it would be level."

Conway stepped off the tractor, scratching his head. Holbrook and the others grinned. Dick elbowed Duba, and Duba nudged Eddie, who winked at Marty.

Conway stepped around in a circle once or twice, thinking. He thought the world of Mary. Had complete respect for her presidency of the Pompey Hollow Book Club. But after all, she was a girl—and he had a notion he could be outdone by a girl, here with an audience and all.

His eyes twinkled. He might save face.

"It sure would lift her up level, you're right there, Mary. But it still would be a front-end heave and it could tilt us over going down," Conway said in a pensive tone, as though he were putting Mary's king in check but being pleasant about it.

"Then just turn the tractor around and back down the hill," she offered, with a checkmate tone in her voice.

Not one to hold a grudge, Conway put his cap back on. "Somebody go hitch her up and bring the hay wagon up here," he barked.

By five o'clock they were all in the cemetery again. The biplane was down in the field next to Big Mike's alfalfa field with a tarp over it. The hay wagon was put back together in the barn where it belonged.

Everyone was proud of Mary's idea that got the plane down safe and sound. She had a right pleasant smile through supper, feeling good about herself, as she should. She knew it wouldn't be long before Eddie could go home to his wife and little girls.

"We're doing the dance and hayride tomorrow night at the Barbers," Mary said.

"That'll be such fun, and a break for you all," Missus said. "We'll call Gertrude and see if we can bring anything."

Ole Charlie here had a few hours before the Angel Congress was to begin. I decided to sit up on the buffet side table and watch my flock enjoy their acorn squash with butter.

CHAPTER 11

THE DICK TRACY CURSE

Leaning in to catch light beams from his dashboard, Dick scribbled notes. He stepped out of the car and made his way over to the gravestone with a lantern light resting on it so he could read if need be. Everyone was sitting around on the ground waiting. Ole Charlie here was up on a pine branch above his head. I still had time before tonight's Angel Congress on Big Mike's barn garage roof was to begin.

"Listen up," Duba barked.

"We'll go through my strategy, first," Dick said. "Then we'll set rules and make assignments. We don't have much time between now and Saturday. You okay with that so far?"

The silence was all the encouragement he needed to push on.

"We're going to catch the bad guys by doing two things," Dick started. "We're planning to pull off both things Saturday and Saturday night—Sunday only if we need to."

"Let's hear it," Marty said.

"We're going to bait a trap to lure the pickpocket in so we can then, in phase two, set him up and catch him red-handed."

"What's red-handed?" Mayor interrupted. "They're always saying 'catch them red-handed.'"

"It means with blood on their hands," Duba said. "In murder mysteries, they get caught in the act—or red-handed."

"Are you two through?" Dick shouted.

"Sorry," Mayor said.

"Second," Dick said, "if there is any chance more people are in on the pickpocketing, we want big bait to bring them all out of hiding and catch them in the same net."

"Smart," Mary said.

"Look at what we know," Dick started.

"Our assets," Duba said.

"We know he's a crook," Dick said. "We know he's a crafty pickpocket…We know he's slick…"

"Check," Duba said.

"And at first, we thought he was Vichy French, but we're not sure now what he is. Tell you later why, but we think he may be an English guy playacting like he's Vichy French to throw us off his trail."

"That's what I think," Duba said. "I think he's a Brit using a phony French accent."

"We're going to hedge our bets," Dick said.

"How?" Mary asked.

"Saturday, Duba and I are going to put on a show on the Midway, starting around noon. We want to draw the pickpocket out. Duba will darken his face, arms and hands—wear earrings. He'll pretend he's like the Gypsies you see in the movies."

"A Hollywood gypsy," Holbrook said.

"He'll be a Gypsy who doesn't understand a word of English or of French either."

"Dumb as a stump," Randy said.

"He'll playact he's a manservant to a rich lady in the wheelchair," Dick said. "I'll be pushing the chair."

"Vichy French cut his tongue out for consorting with the enemy!" Barber said.

Mary poked Barber to hush.

"She's going to be a lady in her wheelchair out getting some sun at the New York State Fair," Dick said.

"Alice!" Mary grinned.

"Alice," Dick said. "She's smart, she knows French or can learn some of it quick enough to get the job done."

"We need to get her a wig so she looks old," Mary said.

"I'll push her wheelchair around the Midway until we get the pickpocket's attention," Dick said.

"I'll be carrying a handful of cash," Duba said. "I'll be running for her whims, buying things—you know, kewpie dolls, ice-cream, cotton candy—spoiling her with state fair junk."

"Me pushing, Duba buying and carrying her packages," Dick said.

"What happens if you set up the lure?" Mary asked.

"Alice will do all the talking."

"You don't know what he looks like," Randy said.

"Eddie does," Dick said. "The pickpocket won't recognize him dressed in bib overalls, red bandanna, and engineer hat. Eddie can find him on the Midway for us and give us a signal."

"For it to work, the pickpocket will have to come to you," Marty said.

"He's right," Tall Jerry said.

"They'll have to smell money," Marty said.

"Are you thinking if Alice sounds Vichy French, the pickpocket will believe her?" Mary asked.

"Believe what?" Marty asked. "I'm still not getting it."

"What aren't you getting, Marty?" Dick asked.

"If Duba, the Gypsy, is carrying all the money in his hand, what good is Alice going to be sitting in a wheelchair the whole time? How can anybody pickpocket her? I don't get it."

"If she'll even do it for us," Dick said, "Alice is going to catch the pickpocket's eye somehow, get him to come to her so she can let him in on her secret."

"Secret?" Marty asked. "What secret?"

"Her counterfeit money printing operation," Dick said.

"I'm intrigued now," Eddie said, sitting up.

"The Hardy Boys and the Secret of the Old Mill," Jerry said. "Those crooks had a secret counterfeit printing press."

"And her counterfeit press will be in my Gypsy wagon," Duba said.

"Hidden up in the woods somewhere," Dick said.

"She'll tell him that she's on to him," Duba said.

"She'll tell him she's been watching him pick pockets and what a waste of time that was for a talent like him," Dick said.

"She'll tell him something like he could be making money—real big money—with her counterfeit cash."

"How's she going to prove anything about any counterfeit money to a pickpocket with nothing more to show than her flapping gums?" Marty asked.

"He's going to want to see something," Mary said.

"She's right," Randy said. "How is she going to put her counterfeit money where her mouth is?"

"What happens if he asks her to prove it?" Holbrook asked.

"That's when she takes bills out of Duba's hand," Dick said. "Her Gypsy manservant hands them to her, and she lifts her blanket to hide them when she fans the counterfeit money out and shows off a wad, just like this."

Dick pulled an inch-thick roll of crisp, new one-dollar bills from his shirt pocket. He removed a rubber band and fanned them out flat like a hand of cards and held them up for all to see.

"She'll show him these new crispy green one-dollar bills, and she'll show him tens and twenties, too. Here, check them out. Pass them around. Feel them. Examine them."

Dick passed the one-dollar bills around to anyone with their hand out.

"This looks real," Mayor said.

"She'll convince the pickpocket he can make big money just by making change for the farmers walking the Midway with hundred-dollar bills in their pockets. Pickpocket takes their real cash folding money and hands the farmers counterfeit bills in exchange," Dick said.

"So, buy counterfeit money from her, real cheap—that'll be her story?" Eddie asked.

"Right," Dick said. "Why should a pickpocket look all day for that one big score when with her counterfeit money, he could get folding cash from anybody walking by?"

"No one would ever know this stuff is counterfeit," Barber said. "It's good."

"If we get caught with this, we're all in the pokey," Randy said. "I don't know if my dad…"

"Okay, there must be a trick to it," Marty said. "How'd you and Duba get counterfeit one-dollar bills?"

"We didn't," Duba said.

"Huh?" Holbrook asked, holding the bills up to the lantern light. "This looks real."

"That's because it is," Duba said.

"These are all real bills," Dick said. "Real US one-dollar bills, but the Vichy French faker will believe whatever Alice tells him they are, and he'll believe they're counterfeit."

"Counterfeit money he can buy cheap and make a fortune by making change," Eddie said.

"Who's not going to believe a lady in a wheelchair who has a Gypsy manservant?"

"Hot dang!" Marty said. "I have lots of questions to answer, lots of detail to work out! My minds a-spinning—but that money sure will work. It had us all fooled, and we're Americans."

"What next?" Barber asked.

"Marty," Duba said, "we'll need a canvas Gypsy wagon, and get with Mrs. Coco—see if she can come up with a costume and makeup for Duba."

"Mary, we need you to come with us to see Alice and help me talk her into this whole thing," Dick said.

90

TALL JERRY AND THE SIDESHOW PICKPOCKET

"If Alice says no, we'll need a new plan," Marty said.

"Meet up here again after school tomorrow, before we go to Barbers for the dance," Dick said. "Marty, have your map of the fairgrounds drawn."

"One hitch," Marty said.

"What?" Dick asked.

"What if the pickpocket wants her to prove the money-changing thing will work?"

"Hadn't thought about that," Dick said. "We'll come up with something by tomorrow's meeting."

They all climbed into the cars going their way and were driven home.

The meeting ended just in time. Ole Charlie here was about to be late getting to my Angel Congress on Big Mike's barn garage roof. I floated up Parker's hill, crossed over and flew straight across to the barn garage at Delphi Falls.

The barn garage roof was aglow when I got to it. Sitting there alone, taking everything in, was a vested, mustached, masterly looking man. Not quite a sneer on his jowls, but a keen eye, sure enough.

I said, "Hello."

"You must be Charlie," the angel said.

"I am, sir, and who might you be?"

"I am Sir Arthur Conan Doyle, Charlie. I'm pleased to meet you."

"Sir Doyle sir, are you who they sent to help me?"

"I am. The understanding is you're having a bit of a go with some Sherlock Holmes theater players, am I correct?" the angel asked.

"One for certain, Sir Doyle. He's handing out Sherlock Holmes theater tickets and stealing people's money, he is for sure."

"That's why I've been asked to come and help you anyway I can."

"Thank you, Sir Doyle."

"Shall we begin?" Sir Doyle asked.

"Sir Arthur Conan Doyle, I could use your advice. I thought you would be best to steer me over some potholes."

Sir Arthur Conan Doyle gave ole Charlie here the once-over. He was pleasant enough about it, but I knew I was getting a checking over.

I didn't know what to say, so I waited.

Sherlock Holmes author Doyle at the Delphi Falls – 1953

"My good man, it'd be a capital mistake to theorize without data," Sir Doyle said. "You proceed first."

"Mr. Doyle, it's been a frightful month. I'm up against women prancing about barely draped, naked calendar girls, and a flock coming to age and all that goes with that."

"Naked bodies, drawings, pictures, and calendars—not an unfamiliar test for the young—for both boys and girls. An ageless challenge, manageable though, quite manageable, I assure you," Sir Doyle mumbled.

"Then there are the pickpockets. Your eminence, we're a country area. Folks here are farmers and growers. They're not in a big city. The pickpockets have come right to our doors, they surely have."

"Certainly, your town have sorts stalking about that you have to keep a watchful eye on, Charlie," Sir Doyle said.

"Oh we have a town drunk, but worst he does is work a day or two on a farm for meals and enough to buy another bottle and then he disappears for days on end."

"Well, there you go."

"Sir Doyle, there are tramps who wander the Cherry Valley hitchhiking – that's Route 20 and they'll stop at local farms and work a day for meals. They're not known for stealing, though. If the food is good, they'll tie a ribbon to a tree limb for other hobo tramps to see."

"It's a nice picture you paint, Charlie, but seems to me you're forgetting about the escaped POWs that stole anything they could get their hands on since the 1940's."

"Oh, my, Sir Doyle. That's right. Sorry, I forgot."

"It was just two weeks ago your flock caught them."

"You're right. Oh well—so we have a dark side too."

"Charlie, the lowest and vilest alleys of London do not present a more dreadful record of sin than does a smiling and beautiful countryside," Sir Doyle said.

"London?" I asked. "That reminds me. There are them Sherlock Holmes player fellas from London, England. I think they're behind the whole mess."

"I'll need more to go on," Sir Doyle said.

"You think the actors are crooks, Mr. Doyle?"

"Well, you have me there," Sir Doyle said.

He twisted his waxed moustache, thinking.

"There are few professions where a person can be King Lear, a world at his feet, a roasted pig hock in his hand one moment, and be a beggar borrowing farthings from a barkeep for a crust of bread, the next. Actors are a whole science all their own."

"You think you can help me, Mr. Doyle?"

"What exactly is heaven's destiny for you, Charles? Have you been given your assignment?"

"One challenge here is a father who was a paratrooper in the war. The pickpockets took his winter money and he almost took his own life as a result."

"He's a parent, is he?"

"Yes. He has two daughters. Can you help?"

"Are the young under your wing are smart, well-meaning and directed?"

"Yes, sir."

"They'll be fine. The paratrooper is disciplined and loving. He'll be fine, too."

"He's a nice lad, sir."

"He'll learn his lesson. Let things take their course. Together they will prevail."

"What about now, sir? What do I do about ladies who tantalize young lads—on calendars and in sideshow Midway tents? They're here, real and today, and in this world, now."

"It's not women who do the tantalizing, Charlie."

"What do you mean?"

"It's the words the barkers use, the sideshow flimflam artists, the publishers who bilk folks of money using man's imaginations by tantalizing them with sinful thoughts."

It was then ole Charlie here thought of what Dick and Duba were putting Tall Jerry through after his seeing the calendar.

"They'll parade women who are trying to put food on the table, Charlie. Think of these women as what they are—these women are respected mothers, daughters, sisters, or aunts—every one of them. Don't paint them with a common 'sideshow barker's' brush. They are God's children. Give your flock proper values about womanhood. That is all they need to see it in a woman's eyes, the mothers, daughters, sisters, and the aunts they are as their first impression. They'll look beyond the circumstance of a moment, or the paint on their faces—just as they looked beyond a horrific war through their childhood."

"I pray for it to work out."

"You're a kind soul, Charlie, and you have a kind flock. Just pray. I'll be here whenever you need me."

"There seem to be bad people around the world, aren't there, Mr. Doyle, sir?"

"My good man, there are those who might be enticed into acting against their nature—into being bad. These types have consciences and might typically be saved in time. But there are those among us who are a devil-born villainous *bad*."

"Can those sorts be changed, Mr. Doyle?"

"Can devil vermin like Moriarty or Hitler be changed, you ask? Only when they were in diapers, I fear."

CHAPTER 12

LATE NIGHT SOS CALLED

In the cemetery, I saw stragglers. Something about their meeting wasn't setting all that well with Marty. He's a detail kind of lad, a mathematical whiz kid. He sensed important details were overlooked and maybe he should step forward before they became big things. Made him a tenacious school newspaper reporter, too.

Dick, Duba, Conway, and Dwyer drove off with most who needed rides. Holbrook, Mary, and Marty were waiting for Mary's dad. Barber was passing time before he walked home.

Watching Marty think I remembered Sir Arthur Conan Doyle telling ole Charlie here that it took a scientist or mathematician to solve a mystery best. Marty was both, and he had an uneasiness in him walking with Mary toward her daddy's car.

"You're the president, Mary," Marty said. "Can I take steps that could help come Saturday?"

"What kind of steps?"

Marty didn't say a word.

Mary saw the concern in his eye. She trusted him.

"Sure, go ahead," she said as she climbed into her daddy's Ford to go home for the first time in days. She needed to rest up before the barn dance tomorrow. Holbrook climbed in behind her.

"Mr. Crane, can you give me a second to tell Barber something?" Marty asked.

"Go ahead, son. We'll wait."

Marty got to Barber before he stepped out of the cemetery for home on foot.

"We need an emergency SOS meeting—tomorrow, noon at Shea's store," Marty said. "Can you call it?"

"For Dick and Duba?" Barber asked.

"For me. Mary says it's okay."

"Okay," Barber said.

"Can you get word out tonight?"

"Pretty late, but I'll do it."

"I need you to call Big Mike, Mike Shea, and Doc Webb, and see if they could be there, too," Marty said.

"You're joking, right?" Barber barked.

This sort of parliament had no precedence. In the history of the Pompey Hollow Book Club, it's never been done before. Mr. Ossant, the agriculture teacher who built props for them, was an exception. Randy's pap, too, who'd pick 'em up and drive them to the Saturday morning picture shows. Mary's daddy would bring Mary to meetings and wait. Big Mike pretty much helped out... and Myrtie. Other than that, adults had never been invited to SOS meetings in the Delphi Falls, the cemetery or Shea's Corner.

"This better be good, Marty, or you're risking consequences by Dick and Duba," Barber warned.

Marty was confident. He had earned his stripes, but he did know SOS meetings were still their call.

The next day, as folks gathered about, by noon the store's front and corner were filled with kids on lunch break waiting for the meeting to start.

Big Mike, Mike Shea, and Doc Webb were in the background, leaning on Big Mike's Oldsmobile.

Marty was inside the store, looking out through the front window. He'd put on a tie and his Sunday coat to make a point that what he had to say was given serious thought. He could see Dick, Duba, Conway, and Dwyer leaning against a maple tree, wondering what was going on. But they were giving him the respect he earned helping them on a few adventures in the past where mercenaries, highwaymen, and crooked varmints were involved.

About then is when he stepped out onto the front steps of the store.

"Listen up," Dick barked, as a courtesy to Marty.

Marty smiled nervously, played with the knot in his tie, twitched his neck.

"Know about the dance and hayride tonight in Barber's barn, do ya?"

Smiles around warmed the crowd, helping him relax.

"The Pompey Hollow Book Club is still meeting today after school before we go to the dance. This meeting isn't replacing that one." Marty thought it best to clear the air, letting people know Dick's meeting was still on.

"In the past, we've had a few weeks to solve something big, right?"

Not certain what he said, the crowd gave his red tie the benefit of the doubt and mumbled and grumbled agreement.

"We have a mission we only have a few days to organize and act on—or we could fail. Show of hands if you're up to it."

Hands in the crowd went up.

"That being settled, I'd like to ask Big Mike, Mike Shea, and Doc Webb to come up and get sworn in."

Well I never…but sure enough, don't ya know, the three of them dressed in their business suits and ties made their way through the crowd, and just as serious as county judges they stepped in front of Marty and stood there, waiting for him to speak.

"Big Mike, Mike Shea, and Doc Webb," Marty started. "We have a mission we'd like to keep secret."

All three raised their right hands in a gesture of understanding.

"Can we ask you gentlemen for something we need and for your trust that we will do our best not to let you down?"

Big Mike had an inkling the mission was to help Eddie, and ole Charlie here figured he'd filled in Mike Shea and the doc while they were leaning on his Oldsmobile. All three nodded their heads.

"We need seven hundred dollars," Marty said.

There was a gasp in the crowd.

"We need two old, crinkly one-hundred-dollar bills and the others in crisp new bills—the new kind like when they stick together."

Not a sound could be heard.

"We need two new hundreds, four new fifties, and the rest can be new twenties or five-dollar bills."

The men stared at Marty in silence.

"I can't tell you why we need them, but we promise it's for a good cause, and we'll try not to lose the money so we can give it all back to you on Sunday, every cent."

It was Doc who broke the spell.

"Bully!" he barked, as though he was Teddy Roosevelt bellowing it. "I'm in."

"We're all in," Mike Shea said.

"It'll be here at the store tomorrow," Big Mike said.

Mouths in the crowd was drop-jaw open. Weren't a soul there ever seen seven hundred dollars before, much less a seven-hundred-dollar decision made so fast it was like buying an ice cream cone.

"Our house didn't cost seven hundred dollars," Holbrook said.

It was a moment to behold, it truly was. Even Dick and Duba and his cohorts admired Marty's spunk and admitted among themselves they had completely forgotten the detail of where they were going to find the money they needed to use as their pretend counterfeit.

Marty wanted to ask the three wise gentlemen to let them plan in secret. But they were young once. They knew.

"If that's about it for us," Big Mike said, "we'll be heading back to work. Good luck."

Mike Shea stepped up and went in the store. Big Mike and the doc made their way through the crowd, got in the Oldsmobile and drove off.

"I have a couple more announcements to make," Marty said. "I'll make them and then turn it over to Dick and Duba."

He had them in the palm of his hand.

"Who plans to be at the State Fair this weekend?"

"Friday is Fair Day. We were going up then," a voice said.

Hands went up.

"Okay, hear this and understand how important it is. Some of us will be in some get-up, maybe in costume on the Midway. Maybe even Alice in her wheelchair. We're not sure who it'll be or what we'll be doing, but we'll be undercover."

"Do you need volunteers?" someone asked.

"Not sure what we need," Dick said from the crowd. "Come to the dance tonight. If we need you, we'll tell you then."

"We're pretty much set," Marty said. "What we need is for you to not recognize us if you see us. Just walk by like you don't know who we are. Can you do that?"

"It'd be easier not to recognize you if we knew who we weren't supposed to recognize, Marty," Mr. Ossant said.

"Fair enough," Marty said. "How about we tell you this tonight at the dance?"

"Who are you trying to catch?" a voice in the crowd asked.

"Eddie, a father with two kids got his winter food money pickpocketed on the Midway. Six hundred and forty dollars he'd earned giving plane rides. He was pickpocketed as he was leaving for home."

"Anything else?" Dick asked.

"That's it for now," Marty said.

Marty caught Dick's eye and sidled over to the maple tree where they were standing.

"Dick, I worried about the money you'll need to make this believable. A few dollars wouldn't do it."

"That was some real thinking, Marty," Dick said.

"I have some ideas," Marty said. "You think about them, and we can meet again in the cemetery before the dance."

"Shoot," Dick said.

"I have a problem with our barging into the Midway Saturday hoping he's there when we don't even know what he looks like. I think you, Duba, and Eddie should go in on Friday to get a look at him, and then we go back Saturday to do our thing," Marty said.

"Good idea," Dick said. "We'll scope it out Friday."

"The fact we don't know for sure if this pickpocket is a Brit or Vichy French, I have a problem using a Gypsy as our lure. During the war the Vichy French locked up thirteen thousand Gypsies, killed off hundreds more."

"What's your point?"

"If this guy is Vichy French, you'd be okay with the Gypsy. I don't know if he'd believe he was mute, though."

"But?"

"Well, if he's a Brit—think about it—won't he have sympathy for the Gypsy and not want to be a part of taking advantage of him like he watched the Vichy French do through the war?"

"Dang," Dick said.

"This is some powerful good strategizing," Duba said.

"What do you have in mind, Marty?" Dick asked.

"Why not let me play a traveling water-witchery—you know, bib overalls, sign hanging around my neck, the whole works. Something like 'WATER WITCHING $50—Book today! Pay today! Guaranteed to find water or you get your money back in FULL!'"

"I thought you were showing Sandy at the horseshow," Tall Jerry said.

"The horse competition is on Friday," Marty replied.

"We only have Saturday anyway, because the Sherlock Holmes players are putting on their show in New Woodstock all day Sunday, and then it will be too late," Dick said.

"What if the pickpocket wants to be careful and check you out first—you know, your water witchery? What do you know about water witchery?" Duba asked.

"I'll have my water witching twig with me, and an apple in my pocket, proving that my twig came from a tree that bears fruit with a seed."

"He knows," Conway said. "Only a water-witcher would know about the seed-bearing fruit."

"That'll do it sure," Duba said.

"I get it," Dick said. "You'll have cash on you that needs changing. You'll be a target for us, right?"

"Better than that," Marty said. "My sign will draw attention that I might have cash. Farmers will ask me for changing their big bills so they can play on the Midway. The water witching will be a front for me—for us. I have a wagon in the woods all right, but it's just something to sleep and eat and travel town to town in."

"Will there be a printing press in it?"

"Think about it. Nobody's going to believe we could print that quality of cash on the spur of the moment in a wagon in the woods. No printing press, I'm suggesting."

"If you don't print the counterfeit, where does the money come from?"

"It'll come from telephone calls to the telephone closet at the Lincklaen House hotel in Cazenovia."

"How'd you pick the Lincklaen House?"

"I saw it once. It has a door so no one can hear you talk. Besides, it'll be convenient to the New Woodstock playhouse where the Sherlock Holmes players will be performing Sunday, and most likely rehearsing Saturday night."

Telephone closet – Lincklaen House – 1953

103

Dick, Duba, Conway and Dwyer sat down, confused.

"The money comes from the telephone closet in the lobby of the Lincklaen House hotel?!" Dick asked.

"Not exactly," Marty said. "I'll be playing the 'fence'—the middleman—for the counterfeit money."

"So, you're not the printer of the money," Dick said.

"'I'm the middleman. Water witching will be my disguise. I don't sell the counterfeit money. I only deliver it to the customer and collect the money. You and Alice are my shills on the Midway. When customers show me cash, proving they have enough to buy the counterfeit and agree to pay COD, that's when I give them a code to use to make the deal."

"I like it," Dick said.

"They wait by that telephone at the time I tell them to. When it rings, they say the code word, agree on the price for the counterfeit they want and the voice on the phone gives them another secret code that they are okay to come to my camp and pay me at my wagon, and that's when they'll get their counterfeit."

"So, who is the mystery voice calling the lobby phone?" Dick asked.

"Myrtie, the telephone operator will make the call for us, disguising her voice," Marty said with a grin.

"When they get to your camp, they pay you first?" Dick asked.

"Maybe I can get them to talk, like confess to what they pickpocketed."

"Holy cow!" Dick said.

"But wait, there's more," Marty said. "Sheriff Todd Hood will be sitting in the back of the wagon listening to the guy buying counterfeit money and confessing. He'll be witness enough to make an arrest."

"One crook to another crook, Myrtie could ask where he stole his money, and could he lay his hands on any more, and he'd probably tell her. Probably brag about it."

"Okay," Dick said, jumping to his feet. "We meet at the cemetery before the dance. Duba, get Alice there. Conway, you go see if you can get Mr. Ossant to come."

Marty felt better now about the small details.

CHAPTER 13

THE PLOT THICKENS

Mary's dad drove in with her, Holbrook, and Randy. Eddie was there, resting back on ole Charlie's marker.

"What are you doing here?" Mary asked.

"I got my chores done, heard about the meeting—decided to come," Eddie said.

"Are you doing okay?"

"I miss my family."

"You'll be home soon. Try to have fun tonight at the dance."

"I'll try. I know the food will be good."

"Plan a jig or two, Eddie."

"I'm not much of a square dancer."

"I have new records," Mary said. "Don't go embarrassing me, making me ask you to dance."

"We'll see," Eddie said.

"Did you call them Sunday?"

"Yes, Big Mike let me use their phone."

"They were thrilled, right?"

"Yes. That only makes it worse."

Mary sat down on the grass. "Tell me about Judy and Lucy."

"How did you know their names?"

"You told me when we were up on the hill looking at your plane that day."

"Seems like forever ago."

"It's all going so fast," Mary said.

"They're seven and five, Judy being seven. She looks most like her mother. Lucy is the tomboy, climbing trees, playing catch."

"Like me," Mary said.

"Lucy is a lot like you, Mary."

"Their daddy's a hero," Mary said.

"The dead guys were the heroes, Mary. We were lucky. But the families, wives and kids know they were heroes who helped save the world."

"That's a nice thought."

"We were young. We knew if we didn't help stop Hitler, the whole world could be doing his goosestep. We wouldn't stand for that."

"The whole world will never forget your paratrooper jump to help save the world."

"I wonder sometimes."

"Someday I'll get lucky and meet a guy like you, Eddie."

"That guy will be the lucky one, Mary."

"Eddie, I want you to listen to me, and listen good."

Eddie raised his head and looked in Mary's eyes, then looked back down at the caterpillar.

"I need the real Eddie to listen, not the pig-headed Eddie."

Eddie looked up and smiled.

"Eddie, in all your life you will never do anything as scary as what you went through then, right?"

"Pretty much."

"Well, we're on a mission now. Only this time nobody will be shooting at us. It may not be as dangerous, but it's as important to us."

"I understand."

"It's important that some guy doesn't get away with this."

"I appreciate—" Eddie started.

"We need to get your money back so Judy and Lucy can have a Santa Claus Christmas like any kid deserves, and you can get your wife a necklace or something for putting up with you."

"I never thought of it that way."

"Of course, you're a man."

"Ha!"

"It's only going to be a few more days when Judy and Lucy look up and see your plane coming in to land in Binghamton that they will hardly remember you even being gone."

"If only that was true."

"It is true, Eddie. I'm a daughter, I know these things."

"You're a wise young lady, Mary."

"Yeah, I know. It's my curse…"

"I don't imagine that would keep boys away."

"And if that isn't enough to run boys off, I can hit a home run, too."

Cars made their way up the cinder drive of the cemetery and emptied out. Eventually two lads lifted Alice out of a pickup and set her wheelchair in front. Ole Charlie here rose to the occasion, sitting on branches over the lot of them.

"Listen up," Duba barked.

"Marty, good job today," Dick said. "We could have blown this whole thing the way we were going about it."

"We were making it so unbelievable it would look like a trap to a crook," Duba said.

"I couldn't sleep thinking about the money thing, the details," Marty said.

"So, here's what we do," Dick said. "Marty's idea. From now on whatever we dream up has got to be believable."

"What we do has to be scrutinized," Duba said.

"We need to get Eddie's money back, so the deeper we want to get into a crook's pocket the more our plans have to pass muster," Dick said.

"That makes sense," Mr. Ossant said.

"Friday is Fair Day at school," Dick said. Have a good time. If you're showing animals or plants or something, Friday is the day they're judging. Duba, Eddie, and I will go on the Midway and see if we can spot the pickpocket. We meet back here Friday night at nine. If we spot him, Saturday will be our D-Day at the state fair, understood?"

They nodded approval.

"On Saturday, when we're doing our thing, nobody can know any of us on the Midway, understood?" Duba asked.

"Mr. Ossant, we need a wagon, nothing fancy, and a team of horses."

"A Gypsy wagon?" Mr. Ossant asked.

"No, this one is a traveling wagon for Orville (Marty) here, and his traveling Water Witchery business."

"So, a buckboard with a canvas top for sleeping?" Mr. Ossant asked.

"That's right," Dick said.

"When do you need it?"

"We'll need it by Saturday midday, so a campfire can be there burning long enough to get a smoke smell in the air and have the char indicating it's been there a while."

Marty beamed a smile, proud of the detail.

"Orville?" Marty asked.

"Make up any name you want, Marty, but let Mr. Ossant know what you come up with so he can put it on the sign on the wagon."

"Jedidiah," Marty said. "I have a business card at the Cortland Carnival. It says Jedidiah. He does séances, you know. He talks to spirits. I'll use that name—Jedidiah."

"We'll need a team of horses," Duba said.

"We need the wagon and horses in the woods somewhere like they've made camp," Dick said.

"Make sure they're unhitched from the wagon and have hay in front of them, so it looks like they've been there some time," Marty said.

"We'll leave cans of food, pots and pans," Mr. Ossant said.

"That will look real," Dick said.

"I have to go to Albany for an FFA conference," Mr. Ossant said. "What do you want me to do with the wagon after it's finished, and I'll need Barber, Dwyer, Conway, and Mayor during school breaks to help build it."

"We'll be there," Conway said.

"I know where I can get my hands on an old buckboard we can rig up with a tarpaulin or a burlap cover," Mr. Ossant said. "That should do the trick."

"A buckboard with a canvas top would be perfect," Marty said.

"Farmer Parker will lend us his horses," Tall Jerry said.

"Take them and the rig into the woods somewhere, and don't forget to draw a map of where it is, so Marty can find it," Dick said.

"That's right," Marty said. "I'll want to look like I'm camping. I'll go to it after we do our thing at the state fair."

"Done," Mr. Ossant said.

"Alice," Dick said, "Duba and I've written a script for you to memorize. Do you think you can act like a tough gal from the city, not afraid of pickpocket varmints?"

"You've never had a roomful of fourth graders."

"That would toughen you," Mary said.

"No, seriously," Alice said. "I was in a play in the seventh grade once and then in my school's senior play. I'll do just fine."

"I'll be the one pushing your wheelchair around the Midway," Dick said. "But you do all the talking."

"You'll tell me who he is?" Alice asked.

"I will, as a matter of fact. To make it look real, if you get to talk with the pickpocket turn your head and tell me to go get some cotton candy or something so you can talk in private."

'Like I'm telling you to get lost, right?" Alice asked.

"That's important," Mary said. "Then you wait for Dick to walk away before you start talking. That'll make it look real."

"Conway—you, Dwyer, and Duba figure out where you'll be loitering on the Midway—don't be together, though," Dick said.

"Two of us will have the old one hundred-dollar bills or new twenties on us. One won't have anything," Duba said.

"Who will have what?" Conway asked.

"We'll figure that out between us who will have the money and where each of us will be standing on the Midway," Duba said.

"Make sure you look like farmers just off from working a field, in overalls," Dick said. "Stand around like you're pondering going into a sideshow or thinking about taking your chances for a kewpie doll before you go to the stock show."

"Best if we have old wallets so nobody gets suspicious with us pulling a hundred-dollar bill from our pocket," Conway said.

Dick took a cigarette from his pack and held it up.

"Conway, Dwyer, and Duba—remember this signal. If you catch my eye, and I have a cigarette tucked over my ear."

He stuck the cigarette over his ear.

"Like this."

"A cigarette over your ear is the signal?" Conway asked.

"Yes, when you see it, whoever is closest to the pickpocket you ask him if he can change a bill for you," Duba said.

"Got it," Conway said. Cigarette over your ear, closest one asks him for change."

"Perfect," Dick said. "Now this is important."

"Go ahead," Conway said.

"If you see him getting close, glance over at me. If I don't have a cigarette over my ear, and he gets close, he's going to be asking you if you can change his small bills into a big one."

"Cigarette over your ear, we ask him. No cigarette we wait for him to ask us, right?"

"Perfect, got it?"

"Yes," Duba, Dwyer, and Conway said.

111

"Now he will get close to each of you, because Alice is telling him how easy it is to convert the counterfeit money into real money. She'll have him trying her scheme."

"And we're the goats," Conway laughed.

"What if I'm the one who doesn't have any money?" Dwyer asked.

"If you don't have any money on you, just say no and walk about your business."

"That will make it look real," Eddie said.

"It won't look rigged if it doesn't go smooth…if someone says no, he's more likely to believe it," Marty said.

"So, here's the deal, Marty," Dick said. "If the pickpocket bites, and Alice does her job of acting like you have a stash of counterfeit for sale, he will come up to you and want to do business."

"I'll be ready," Marty said.

"You brush him off the first time, Marty, like—'Who are you?' or 'Go away, mister, you're bothering me. I don't know what you're talking about.'"

"I gotcha," Marty said.

"That sort of thing," Dick said. "But when he comes at you again, you ask if he knows the Lincklaen House in Cazenovia. Whisper to him you don't sell it, you only deliver it."

"That's perfect," Marty said.

"Ask him what time he can be there. Give him a code word to use and tell him to be in the lobby phone closet at the time he says."

"Any code word?" Marty asked.

"Any code word," Dick said. "Just be sure when you leave the Midway you pick up a phone somewhere and tell Myrtie the word and the time she has to call the Lincklaen House phone closet."

"Gotcha," Marty said.

"Marty," Mr. Ossant said. "Rehearse some chatter so you'll feel comfortable prancing around the Midway selling your water witchery services."

"Don't forget your apple," Conway said.

"Mr. Ossant, make sure you leave three copies of a map to the camp with the front desk clerk at the hotel Saturday," Marty said. Leave them in envelopes, one for me, one for 'Sherlock Holmes' and one for Sheriff Todd Hood. That way the sheriff will know where the camp is and can go arrest the pickpocket."

"Will do," Mr. Ossant said. "Three copies."

"I wouldn't mark one for Sheriff Todd Hood," Dick said. "That could spook the pickpocket if he sees it. How about 'Messenger'?"

"I'll mark the third one to Messenger," Mr. Ossant said.

"We'll see you here Friday night for a final go-through," Dick said. "Rehearse as much as you can until then."

"Meeting adjourned," Dick said.

"Let's go dance," Mary said.

CHAPTER 14

BARN DANCE

You should know this is the way it was in the Crown in 1953. There were reasons country folk could be counted on to drop what they were doing and come by without an invite.

Someone dying was one.

They'd come miles for a wake. Walk, if they had to. Ladies with hats on, men holding theirs over their heart—circling the yard, waiting to take their sympathies inside, maybe a cheery word or two like 'don't he look nice,' or- 'ain't her dress purdy, though.'

Second reason they'd come uninvited was if your barn burned.

Barns could burn for reasons bigger than dropping a lantern or a crack of lightning. Greener hay can sometimes smoulder under a pile of dry hay and spontaneously combust—blaze up on its own accord. They had barn raisings in two days, to save the farm, and neighbors would come. Day one was getting the first rafter up, fixing that with the pulley for hefting all the rafters. Day two was putting up the siding and roofing.

Third reason was to dance.

Tonight was special to ole Charlie here as Sir Doyle made it an honor by accepting my invite to witness something he'd never seen. He'd never seen an American square dance.

We could talk angel shop, if'n he had a mind to, but tonight was more about watching from the roof, enjoying the sights and sounds.

"Mr. Doyle, sir, the fire they're building in the rock pit will reach the heavens. Takes full-time watching to keep her safe but she is a spectacle."

"Charlie, old salt, is the fire a sign of festivities?"

"This time of year, it's mostly to get warm, I reckon."

Carl Vaas's milk-can hauling truck pulled in the drive and parked under a tree on the side. Its door busted open and out poured half a dozen young'uns, Randy leading the pack.

Seeing them, Mrs. Barber waved and stepped off the porch with a dishtowel in her hand. Judy Clancy was standing by a tree, picking up a chicken drumstick from her paper plate while catching up with Alice, Mary Margaret Cox, Judy Finch, Linda, and some others waiting for the dance to begin.

"Judy," Mrs. Barber said. "Dear, if you see your Jimmy, would you tell him Mr. Barber would like to see him and the boys up at the house."

"He's helping set up Mary's record player. What boys?"

"You know, the SOS boys—Dick, Duba, your Jimmy, of course, and Dwyer," Mrs. Barber said.

"Are they in any kind of trouble, Mrs. Barber?"

"No, dear, nothing like that. Mr. Barber wants to chat a spell. Will you see they come to the house?"

"Yes, ma'am," Judy said.

It didn't take long for word to spread to Dick and the boys. It also spread through the Pompey Hollow Book Club. When the time came, Jerry, Holbrook, Randy, Mayor, Bases, Barber, Marty, and Mary followed the older boys over to the house.

Mary was met at the door by Mrs. Barber.

"Honey, why don't you take this piece of apple pie and go see about getting the music started?"

"But…" Mary started.

"Everybody's here who's coming tonight by the look at all the cars, I'm thinking, and they've all eaten mostly," Mrs. Barber said.

"But…" Mary started.

"There's more food if they want it. It's time for some dancing. The boys will be down soon enough," Mrs. Barber said.

"Can't I go in with them?" Mary asked.

Mrs. Barber took Mary aside.

"I think this is a man-talk sort of thing, Mary."

"What do you mean?"

"Best you go get people settled and the music started. They'll be along shortly."

Mary stepped off the porch scratching her head. She turned and walked over to where Eddie and Hal were standing and talking. She handed little Bobby the paper plate and piece of pie.

"Mary, Hal here has been telling me how you guys protected Bobby all summer so he could be with his dad. I think I'm going to owe you a big apology for not putting faith in your intentions straight off. I've given you a hard time."

Mary held her hand out and took Bobby by one hand.

"We did what you'd do—or most anybody, for that matter," Mary said. "We took a kid out of harm's way. He was sleeping in an alley and we gave him a bed and a tub until his daddy could come and raise him proper. Isn't that right, Bobby?"

Bobby looked up with a bit of pie crust on his lip and smiled. Mary stroked the boy's hair with the tips of her fingers, looking for a part.

Inside the house, ole Charlie here and Sir Doyle were in the dimly lit room as the young men drifted in and stood in front of the table. Mr. Barber, Big Mike, Doc Webb, and Mike Shea were already there, smiling, but the lads sensed they were either on trial or about to learn something.

"We only wanted to see the older boys," Mr. Barber said. "You younger boys don't need to stay."

"We're all in this together," Dick said.

"We can take it," Randy said.

"Okay, fellas," Mr. Barber said.

Mr. Barber sat down.

"I've been asked to be the talker for what we have to say, so bear with me. I'm a farmer's son and not a preacher or public speaking politician. Be patient."

"You're doing fine," Big Mike said.

Dick, Duba, and the boys looked at their adversaries, checking for some sign, something in the eyes. They could only see smiles.

"What's the count, Big Mike?" Mr. Barber asked.

Mike Shea was ahead of them on face count.

"All told, there are eleven of them here," Mike Shea said.

With that Mr. Barber reached down into his pocket deep enough to pull out a roll of dollar bills. He fanned them out, and handed the money over to the doc.

"Doc, what say you give two dollars each to the fellas here, and then we'll get started," Mr. Barber said.

"Bully!" the doc bellowed. He walked around the table and handed each lad two one-dollar bills. He stepped to the side of the table with the gents.

"What'd we do to deserve this?" Dick asked.

"I'm not looking a gift horse in the mouth," Duba said.

"Hold on fellas, I'm fixin' to tell you," Mr. Barber said. "You boys get your folding money?"

"Yup," Holbrook said.

"You're a good lot," Mr. Barber said. "Folks in the Crown would agree that's a pretty fair statement."

"They are," the doc said.

"Other than the drag racing from Hasting's down Oran Delphi when a body's sleeping, you're pretty much the sorts we can be proud of," Mr. Barber said.

"And when you're proud of someone you want to favor it in any way you can, to help them through life a bit more," Mike Shea said.

"It'd be selfish not to," the doc said.

"You don't have to pay us," Conway said.

"We do stuff because we want to," Dick said.

"It's not *pay*," Big Mike said.

"It's more like a life learning experience," Mike Shea added. "We know there's been talk about what some of you are up to at the fair."

"Consider us giving it a push," Big Mike said.

"Catching the pickpocket?" Dwyer asked.

"You already gave us money to do that," Conway said.

"This isn't about the pickpocket," the doc said.

"Huh?" Conway asked. "What, then?"

"Fellas, fellas," Mr. Barber said. "We gave you the two dollars because we want you to have enough to go see the hoochie-coochie girls at the State Fair, like you want to."

"The money will be enough to get you in," Big Mike said.

"Might as well sow your oats—get it out of your systems," Mike Shea said.

"What!?" Conway snorted. "I wasn't going to any girlie show. I wouldn't hurt my Judy for the life of me."

"My ma would tan me sure," Randy said. "I'd never go."

"It only costs a dollar," Holbrook said. "You gave us two."

"A dollar is for the popcorn," Big Mike said.

"You're kidding, right?" Duba asked.

"There's some catch to this," Dwyer said.

Dick was getting the message.

"I think I know what is going on," he said. "Somehow you heard we were going to the girlie show and you want us to know you knew."

"What do you mean, 'we,' Dick?" Mayor asked. "I wasn't..."

"Tain't it, son," Mr. Barber said. "But go on with what you were saying."

"Maybe we were thinking it—gave it some notion—but that was then and now is now," Dick said.

"You want to put that in English, son?" Mike Shea asked.

"It's different now, is all," Duba said.

"We've been so busy planning how we can help Eddie, we haven't had time to even think about the girlie show," Dick said.

"Matter of fact we already decided helping him was probably more fun anyway, and we weren't going to go," Duba said.

"So, what you're saying is maybe it's better you boys stay busy with life's important things and not be idle, thinking too much on distractions?" Mr. Barber asked.

"I want it on the record, I was never going," Conway said.

"This ain't a court, son," Mr. Barber said.

"What did you mean, 'we,' Dick?" Mayor barked.

The lads looked at the two dollars in their hands, silent, some letting their imaginations keep their state fair options open.

"It's only a dollar," Holbrook said. "Not that I was going to go."

"I wouldn't disrespect my sister or my mother by going to that sort of thing," Randy said.

"I won't lie," Mayor said. "I first figured I'd be afraid the whole world would see me going in or coming out of the hoochie-coochie show. That alone scared me from thinking about it. But then I started to think that if I was scared, I'd be seen, it must be no good for me to begin with, so I stopped thinking about it altogether."

"That's called a conscience," Marty said.

Mr. Barber smiled.

"That thinking is sure enough called 'character,' son," Mr. Barber said.

In the background the music and square dance calling started up. The lads were getting edgy.

"Like we said," Dick said. "Sure, we thought of going, but we got busy helping Eddie and forgot about it. Keep your money. We're not going."

With that Dick and Duba laid their two dollars on the table in front of the men standing there. The rest of the lads followed suit, stepping around and placing the money on the table.

"We're not worried about a growing lad and their curiosity in worldly temptations—in a world that is painted and perfumed to lure the unsuspecting," Mr. Barber said.

"You've now about said you are, for the most part, with the character it takes to keep on the straight and narrow," the doc said.

"We were never worried about your stepping too far off course," Big Mike said.

"Why I never seen a better group of youngsters in my life," Mike Shea said.

"You've all proved it to me," Big Mike said.

"So, why are we here?" Duba asked.

"It's stealing that ain't right," Mr. Barber said.

"Huh?" Conway asked.

"Word was you were planning to sneak in under a tent at the Midway without paying for a ticket," Big Mike said.

"We tried to teach you well," Mr. Barber said. "We taught you respect for someone's property, and that stealing was never a way of life."

"Mr. Barber, we've caught crooks," Holbrook said. "Since we were nine, we've been catching them. They're the ones who steal."

"Now we're going to catch a pickpocket," Mayor said.

"You slip under a tent, get away with not paying for a ticket, you're no better than a pickpocket or some burglars sneaking into stores at night," Mike Shea said.

"We never thought of it that way," Dick said.

"What do you mean, we?" Mayor snarled.

"Go have fun," Mr. Barber said. "Go on now, git!"

The dining room emptied, young men tripping over each other getting out. Holbrook and Jerry stepped off the porch, each with a piece of pie in their hand.

"Why did you keep saying the tickets to the girlie show were only a buck?" Jerry asked.

"You told me to find out how much it cost, and I asked is all," Holbrook said. "What's the big deal?"

"Well now the whole world knows we were thinking of going," Jerry said.

"Look. We gave them the two dollars back, didn't we?" Holbrook insisted. "They know we're not going."

"That's not the point," Jerry said.

"You mean we are going?"

"No, that's not what I said."

"What are you saying?"

"I mean we considered going for purely scientific reasons, not for the other, well, you know…"

"I think that *is* the point," Holbrook said.

"What's that supposed to mean?"

"Neither one of us know, and we thought going to a girlie show would answer some questions we had—you know—about girls," Holbrook said.

"It was purely scientific," Jerry insisted.

"I'm not good with English, Tall Jerry, but I don't think I'd use the word *purely* in a sentence about us going to a girlie show."

"Know what I wished?"

"What?"

"I wished when kids joked all summer about going skinny-dipping, somebody actually did—go skinny…ya know."

"Know what I wish?" Holbrook asked.

"What?"

"I wished you never saw that naked girl calendar. You haven't been the same since," Holbrook said.

"Well, they're not the same," Jerry said.

"Who's not the same?"

"Girls and boys."

"Well, yeah! Welcome to the real world," Holbrook said. "Girls have to wear brassieres for a reason, ya know."

121

"I know that, but they don't have something else that boys do," Jerry whimpered.

"What are you talking about?"

"They don't have a thingy."

Holbrook slugged Jerry on the arm.

"A what?!"

"A thingy."

"Shut up."

"I didn't see one on the calendar."

Holbrook slugged Jerry again.

"Shut up."

"How do they pee without a thingy?" Jerry asked.

"I have a lot of sisters, stupid. Trust me they pee, and they tie up the bathroom all morning sometimes."

Holbrook wasn't into starting a great debate with his naïve best friend here at a square dance social. There'd be plenty of time later for young Jerry to learn about girls and get his ears wrung out, he thought.

"Let's go see if Judy Finch, Mary Margaret or Donna are dancing yet," Holbrook said. "Let's dance with somebody."

"Head lady and first gentleman forward and back…
forward again with both hands round."

And dance they did.

Mary's new record was the Virginia Reel square dance. Eddie danced and Hal danced. Duba took Alice's wheelchair with her in it and did a jig, spinning her about the floor, grinning to a lively tune. People clapped and cheered. It was a wonderful night.

Sir Doyle and I rose up and sat on the roof, taking it in.

"Did you enjoy yourself tonight, Sir Doyle? Best an angel is allowed, that is?"

"Why I've never seen such a clever plot to get growing pain issues on the table and discuss them without a word of lecture," Sir Doyle said. "I'm impressed with what I've seen here in America. I certainly learned many things tonight, Charlie my friend."

"I'm pleased and hope you'll come back, Sir Doyle." "Something tells me you're here for other reasons that ain't come up yet."

"I've had the same premonitions," Sir Doyle, said. "Time will tell."

CHAPTER 15

FAIR DAY

Fair Day Friday meant no school. Pupils got the day to visit the fair or enter livestock or crops in state fair competitions.

Dick, Duba, Conway each drove separately, cars filled with kids. Mr. Vaas and other parents loaded as well, and drove early enough to be at the ticket booth opening. They pulled into the fairgrounds parking areas like a Patton tank division. Dick asked club members to wait by the car while they decided their approach to scoping things out—getting a lay of the land.

"Where's Marty?" Dick asked.

"Where's Marty?" Duba asked.

"He's not here," Randy said.

"What?!" Dick growled. "He has the fairground map."

"Hold your shorts," Holbrook said. "Marty's already here. He's showing Sandy today."

"He was supposed to give me a drawing of the fairground," Dick said.

"Marty gave me his satchel so I could give his map to you. Hold on, I have it somewhere," Holbrook said.

"Where's Mary?" Dick asked.

"She went to Barbers' to help pick up from the dance," Tall Jerry said.

"We're falling apart here," Duba moaned.

Holbrook pulled a drawing of the fairgrounds from Marty's leather satchel and handed it to Dick.

Dick stepped to the front hood of his car and unfolded it.

"Here's where we are," Duba said, placing his finger on the map.

"Eddie, you stick with us," Dick said. "Leave your leather flight jacket here."

Duba handed Eddie a jean jacket to wear.

"The rest of you, go have fun," Dick said. "We'll meet you in the car show at noon for a report."

"If you're not there, we're not looking for you," Duba said.

"For sure be at the cemetery tonight by nine," Dick said.

"But we stay off the Midway, right?" Randy asked.

"No Midway," Duba said.

"We might get lucky. Maybe Eddie can point the pickpocket out right off," Dick said.

"I'll walk in the middle of you and Duba," Eddie said to Dick.

Studying the map, then folding it up, Dick, Duba, and Eddie started milling with the crowd toward the entrance.

"Eddie, if we spot the guy, I think you should head back, so we don't risk your being seen," Dick said.

Duba stepped up to the ticket booth.

"Lady, tomorrow we have a friend coming in a wheelchair," Duba said.

"Okay," the ticket lady said.

"One of us will have to come out to get her, would you let us back in with the same ticket?" Duba asked.

"You'll need new tickets for Saturday," the ticket lady said. "This ticket is only good for today."

"I'll have a new ticket tomorrow."

"Come to me tomorrow. I'll let you come out and take your friend in."

My-oh-my, what a wonder the New York State Fair was for ole Charlie here. Why, there were tall camels cantering in long stride following a man wearing a turban to the rear of a tent. A tiger was prancing back and forth in a wagon cage.

"They have a circus show in the main arena the night they close the fair down," Dick said.

The rabbit exhibit was filled with cages, stacked taller than a body could see over, rabbits of all kinds and colors. There were Netherland Dwarf rabbits, Holland Lop rabbits, Dutch rabbits. Tall Jerry's friend from down past the doc's on Cardner Road, Paul Shaffer was sitting on the stage in his Sunday best, waiting for the judges to get to his cages. He usually won the blue.

Marty was sitting proper in the saddle, riding Sandy into the ring. They stopped and turned with the palomino's snow-white mane flying. A golden beam of the sun through the roof portals glowed down on the pair. Win or lose, Sandy was the prettiest horse. Scratchy voices on the sound system echoed throughout the great hall. People walked about shaking hands in pathways between stables, kennels and cages, wishing each other luck.

The food pavilion was quiet inside. Seems there's a religion to cooking, canning, and preserves. Mrs. Parker stood over her quarts of butter pickles, catching up with old friends, with not a care in the world if she won a ribbon or not.

Behind the food pavilion was the elephant tent. Six elephants with chains around their ankles ripped bales of hay apart with their trunks, one snorting a bugle after seeing Dick, Duba, and Eddie walk by.

The tin flute, snare drum, and clapping cymbals of calliope music celebrated the merry-go-round, while the tic-tic-tic-tic-tic sounds of spinning fortune wheels tapped through the air. Noises reminiscent of the annual fair and its sights and sounds let Dick and Duba know they were close to the Midway and the beginning of an adventure.

"Let's slow down, guys," Dick said. "Eddie, keep your head low but your eyes peeled."

Turning the corner onto the Midway a sideshow talker spotted them by his tent. Sure enough, it was the *hoochie-coochie* tent. The talker leaned down from the stage, and with a white and red-striped cane he gently poked Dick on the shoulder. The talker was wearing red garter belts at his elbows on his sleeves and a flat straw skimmer hat tipped to the side.

"Tell ya' what I'm going to do!" the talker barked. "Step right up, gentlemen, and I was certain you were gentlemen the minute I laid eyes on you rounding the corner."

Dick, Eddie, and Duba stopped in front of the man on the stage pointing his cane at them.

"Why this is your lucky day, gentlemen. Step in close and look behind me. It happens that hidden by that curtain is something only bonafidee' gentlemen with worldly experience would appreciate."

Dick and Duba stood gaping up at the stage, jaws dropped. Eddie moved his eyes around the Midway.

"Step in folks, for I'm going to give you a free look at pulchritude magnificence that caused unnamed men in Paris to have to change their names. Behind that curtain is a lady— don't worry, gentlemen, I'm going to give you a free peek—a lady so bejewelled with strands so elegant, pearls so opulent they're under armed guard whenever she isn't letting gentlemen like you up close and personal to watch her take each and every one of them off in front of your eyes, revealing her other qualities."

Duba elbowed Dick in the ribs.

"Get my meaning, gentlemen? And she takes them all off, yes-sir-ree, every delicate strand, every little white pearl. Use your imagination. Be careful if you have a bad heart. We can't be responsible."

"Dick," Eddie said.

Dick couldn't take his eyes off the curtain behind the talker.

"Dick," Eddie said, nudging him.

Dick turned his jaw to speak to Eddie while keeping his eyes locked on the talker and the curtain. "Hold on," he said.

"Step up, gentlemen, and I'll share a secret with you. When the pearls come off, she starts up around the milk barn and she winds up down near the hen house. Why gentlemen, I'm going…"

"Hey, Dick!" Eddie barked, poking him in the ribs. "I see the guy!"

"Huh?" Dick turned.

"Over there by the third tent. I see the guy," Eddie said.

"Where?" Duba asked.

They stepped away from the crowd closing in around the beauteous-bevy-of-Parisian-ladies talker.

"Count the tents," Eddie said.

"Across the Midway?" Dick asked.

"Yes, three tents over," Eddie said.

"Got it," Dick said.

"See the guy in the beret and the seersucker coat?"

"Flower in his lapel?" Dick asked.

"Carnation, red," Eddie said.

"Okay," Dick said. "I see him."

"Where?" Duba asked.

"Shut up and turn around," Dick said.

"Let's get out of here," Eddie said.

"Back out slowly before he sees us," Dick said.

"Let's go find the kids," Eddie said.

Dick and Eddie made it around the side of the tent before they realized Duba was still listening to the talker. Dick's arm reached around the corner of the tent, grabbed Duba and yanked.

Eddie had sweat on his brow, angry he couldn't walk up to the red carnation and bust him in the nose.

"It's too early to meet the kids," Dick said, looking at his watch.

"They'll find rides," Duba said. "They'll figure we had to leave."

They first drove to Mr. Ossant's shop at school to see how the wagon was coming, so they could report at tonight's cemetery meeting.

CHAPTER 16

FRIDAY THE 13TH

"Alice, are you ready for tomorrow?" Dick asked.

"You being a wise guy or something, hot shot? Don't let this wheelchair fool you, slick. I can still kick your butt, or have it done for me. Get lost...take a powder...How's that?" Alice asked.

"Wow!" Mary sparked.

"Perfect," Dick said.

Alice grinned.

"Marty?" Dick asked.

Marty stood and turned.

"Folks, farming's tough enough with water, but impossible without it. Cows need water, chickens need water—follow Jedidiah to the water."

Marty held up his water witchery branch.

"With Jedidiah you're drinking from your own well in a week, watering crops or your money back. Who needs water, folks?"

He pointed at Mary. "Need water, ma'am?"

He pointed at Eddie. "How about you, sir? Jedidiah knows where the water is."

"That was good," Eddie said.

"Duba, pretend you're the pickpocket," Marty said.

"What?" Duba asked.

"Go on, pretend you're the pickpocket. Ask me if we can do business. Go on, ask."

"Hey, buddy," Duba growled. "I want some counterfeit. Can we do business?"

"I'm a Water Witcher, mister, just trying to earn a living. Don't know what you're talking about."

"You've got it, Marty," Mary said. "Good job."

"Duba, Conway, and Dwyer, have you figured out where you guys will be loitering?" Dick asked.

"I'll be in front of the girlie-show tent," Conway said.

"I'll be at the freak-show tent, or maybe throwing baseballs," Duba said.

"I'll be at the target range," Dwyer said.

"Watch for the signal—the cigarette over my ear," Dick said.

"How are we going to know who the pickpocket is?" Marty asked.

"You'll see us talking to him."

"Then what do we do?" Marty asked.

"Slow down," Duba barked.

"Sorry," Marty said.

"We'll get to it," Duba said.

"You guys standing around just act natural," Dick said.

"Like we shouldn't stare at you, but we should keep an eye out for…" Conway started.

"Watch for my signals," Dick said. "If I have a cigarette over my ear, whoever is closest to the pickpocket ask him if he can change a bill. If I don't have a cigarette over my ear and he gets close, it means he's going to be asking if you can change his small bills into a big one."

"Eddie?" Duba asked. "Does your biplane have a two-way radio on it? A shortwave?"

"Yes, it does."

"Turn it on come dark tomorrow night. Sheriff Hood will be at Myrtie's, the telephone operator's place. You can listen in."

"Does Myrtie have shortwave?" Randy asked.

"She has to when wires are down, so she can report it."

"Anything else?" Duba asked.

"One thing," Mr. Ossant said. "I can't get Farmer Parker's horses until after two o'clock tomorrow, but he said we can keep them all night if we need them."

"Midday," Marty said. "That'll work."

"We won't be leaving the fair until later, when we see the pickpocket leave," Dick said.

"When I get the horses, I'll take the wagon deep into the woods somewhere in Pompey Hollow," Mr. Ossant said.

"Make sure to draw maps to the camp and leave them at the Lincklaen House, like we said," Dick said.

"We'll tie the horses, so they'll be safe. They'll have plenty of hay, but I won't start a fire. We'll be heading to Albany and don't want to leave a fire burning in the woods unattended."

"Who's we?" Duba asked.

"Farmer Parker will be following me and the wagon to the camp in my car, and then he's riding with me to Cazenovia where we'll drop off three maps."

"Why don't I go with them," Tall Jerry asked.

"Why?" Dick asked.

"I can get a fire going and make coffee and cook stuff while we're waiting," Jerry said.

"What do you think, Eddie?" Dick asked.

"If the pickpocket shows up at the camp, two guys shouldn't spook him," Eddie said.

"Marty and I can be playing pitch, rolling dice or something when he comes," Tall Jerry said.

"You don't drink coffee," Dick said.

"We'll look older if we're drinking from coffee tins."

"Okay," Dick said. "When Marty gets there, you two play it by ear."

"Tall Jerry, you hide out away from the camp if you think you have to," Duba said.

"We'll see how it goes," Jerry said.

"Marty, as soon as we handle our business on the Midway—and after he's tested making change and you've done your act," Dick started, "Conway will be waiting for you at the entrance. Head to the Lincklaen House, get your copy of the map and go to your camp."

"Help finish setting up camp like you've been there awhile," Duba said.

"Will do," Marty said.

"The wagon will have pots, pans, and canned goods," Mr. Ossant said.

"Conway, don't stop anywhere. We don't want Marty seen and recognized by the Sherlock Holmes actors," Dick said.

"I won't."

"Drop him off on the roadside like you just gave him a ride like a hitchhiker and drive on," Dick said.

"I got it," Conway said.

"Marty, find the camp using your map," Dick said.

"Anything else?" Duba asked.

"Mike Shea thought maybe you might need this," Mr. Ossant said, stepping forward.

He handed Dick an envelope with the money in it. Dick slapped his forehead.

"This whole thing is nerve-racking," Dick said.

"And these," Mr. Ossant said, handing Dick the state fair passes for all the crew.

"The devil's in the details," Marty said.

"Can Barber, Randy, and I catch a ride up to the fair with somebody tomorrow?" Mary asked.

"Ride with us," Eddie said.

"Eddie, after you drop us off tomorrow, keep my car," Dick said.

"Do I wait for you?" Eddie asked.

"No," Dick said. "Randy, you go with Eddie. Show him how to get back."

"Gotcha," Randy said.

133

"Anybody who wants to hear the sheriff through shortwave, meet at my plane."

"Circle around," Dick said. "Hold hands."

They did.

"Mary, you're the best at it," Dick said. "Give us a prayer that we get Eddie's money back."

There was a sense of how important the next twenty-four hours could be in the lives of a family. Those in the circle had known tough times at one time or another.

"Dear God, please help us do right tomorrow so Lucy and Judy can have a Christmas, and they can break bread as a family, and Eddie can stay home and be a painter. I don't know what to say, God, but you know. Please help us, amen."

Mary looked at Eddie. "Eddie, are you crying?"

Eddie dropped his head.

"Don't cry, Eddie. We're going to get your money back."

"My platoon of paratroopers held hands and prayed before we boarded the plane."

Mary reached and took Eddie's hand and squeezed it.

"It's all going to work out," she said.

The meeting broke up, tires crunched in the dark down the cinder drive of the cemetery.

Ole Charlie here was about to be prayerful when I heard the voice talk to me, clear as anything.

"You did well, Charlie. You did well, my friend."

It was Sir Doyle, for sure.

"Don't I have a nice flock, Sir Doyle?"

"You certainly do, Charlie. The big day is tomorrow."

"It looks like they're ready, Sir Doyle."

"I'll say a prayer, my friend."

CHAPTER 17

THE DAY OF RECKONING

"Mrs. Parker, you have the best bacon," Randy said.

"Our hogs are mostly corn-fed—crab apples and silage, too," Mrs. Parker said. "We hickory smoke once a year."

"I like that you have thick slices," Randy said.

"I'm going to miss your home cooking, Mrs. Parker," Eddie said. "I tasted your butter pickles at the dance."

"We know you have a big day planned in Syracuse at the State Fair. Just please be careful," Mrs. Parker said.

"They'll be careful," Eddie said. "They've planned it out pretty good."

"Myrtie would like you to come to supper," Mrs. Parker said.

"In New Woodstock?" Randy asked.

"At her place, yes," Mrs. Parker said. "Sheriff Hood will be there waiting for a signal to go arrest the pickpocket."

"Will you come, Eddie?" Randy asked.

"She's counting on you all coming," Mrs. Parker said.

"I'll go," Eddie said.

"Mrs. Parker?" Tall Jerry asked. "Did you live in the Great Depression?"

"Tall Jerry, sweetheart, it was more like nobody 'lived' in the Depression—but somehow we managed to live through it," Mrs. Parker said.

"Did you have the farm, or did you go hungry?" Randy asked.

"We were just getting started and learned to go without. I could make a chocolate layer cake in the '40s with everything but chocolate."

"Things will be tight for Eddie if we don't..." Holbrook started.

"Hush!" Mary snapped.

"Eddie, if you fly back here, don't you be landing on top of the hayfield hill," Marty said with a chuckle.

"Hey, Marty," Mary said, "I like your hat and suspenders. You ought to have a piece of straw hanging from your mouth. Are you going to wear shoes or go barefoot?"

"I want to look hayseed, but not too huckleberry. I have old boots my dad's worn holes in. I got me a burlap shoulder-strap bag for my witching twig and the apple."

"A regular Johnny Appleseed," Randy said.

"I got the idea for it out of a library book. I saw a sketch of the one Johnny Appleseed carries," Marty said. "Mom sewed it."

"Are you ready, Alice?" Dick asked.

"Let's see the color of your money, wise guy. I don't waste no time on any two-bit flimflam artist. Show me the green or get lost, buddy...how's that?" Alice asked.

"Perfect," Dick said.

"Good heavens," Mrs. Parker said.

"You like it, for real?" Alice asked.

"Sounds real to me, like the streets of a big city—like in the movies," Conway said.

"That's such a relief," Alice said. "I've never been so scared in all my life."

Dawn was breaking, so the bunch of 'em walked down to the barn to say hello to Farmer Parker while he was finishing his milking. The barn was lighted with friendly bulbs hanging and warm with smells of the new lofted hay and warm, fresh milk in cans. The radio was tinkling out a player piano-roll tune introducing the morning's wake-up farm report.

136

"Eddie?" Farmer Parker asked while looking up from his stripping a cow.

"Yes, sir," Eddie said.

"Heard you might need to go to the fair to help 'em out. That'd be fine. You go do what you have to do."

"Thanks," Eddie said. "I'm driving some up. I want to be there in case they need help."

"Eddie, I decided I'm staying here with Mrs. Parker," Mary said.

"Why?" Randy asked.

"I'm going to help make salad and things for Myrtie's supper tonight. I saw the fair yesterday and I'd be a bundle of nerves worry-wart there today."

"Eddie, does the biplane take a regular octane or is there an oil mix to it?" Farmer Parker asked.

"Regular. Any octane is good. I usually buy the cheapest," Eddie said.

"Well, you'll find four five-gallon cans of gas setting next to your plane when you get back from dropping them off. Regular octane. We'll get more if need be to fill the tank."

"That's mighty nice of you," Eddie said.

"You've earned it, son," Farmer Parker said. "That was our deal."

"Thank you, my friend," Eddie said.

"The Mrs. and I were beginning to favor having you around."

"You're good people," Eddie said.

"The gas cans have to go back to Hasting's store when they're empty."

"I'll take them," Barber said. "When I go home later tonight, I'll take them. Someone's picking me up."

"My dad could haul them, if you want," Randy said. "He goes right by the store."

Ole Charlie here was making notice how chatty and jittery young souls in this old dairy barn was being this morning. Why, the last time I saw these sorts of nerves I was waiting in line to get

137

my angel wings that time I learned I was going to be guardian angel to this flock. I couldn't read more than a measuring yardstick. Not being able to spell *guardian angel* is what was making me a nervous, jittery wreck first day up. How would I ever know what line to get in if there were signs naming the lines?

Conway pulled in the drive, loaded Alice's wheelchair in his truck and lifted her into the cab.

They headed for Syracuse and the state fair. As they reached the fairgrounds each vehicle waited in the parking lot for the next. Conway stood behind Duba's pickup, counting heads.

"Have fun," Dick said, "but today you don't know Marty, you don't know me, you don't know Conway, you don't know Duba, and you don't know Dwyer or Alice, get it?"

"We get it," Barber said.

"Tall Jerry and I are going to see the wild animals," Holbrook said.

"If you see any of us, just walk on by," Duba said.

"And if you see any other kids from school, tell them, too," Dick added.

Dick turned to Eddie.

"Eddie, we've been thinking."

"What about?" Eddie asked.

"We need you to take Randy and head back here," Dick said.

"To Delphi Falls?" Eddie asked.

"We can't take the chance of them seeing you," Dick said. "They may be on the lookout."

"Probably a good idea," Eddie said. "Crooks are always on the lookout for trouble."

"Are you okay with coming back?" Dick asked.

"I'm good. Just give me directions," Eddie said.

"I'll come back with you," Randy said. "I'll show you how to get back."

"Take my car up and back," Dick said.

He threw Eddie the keys.

"We'll double up. I'll ride with Duba," Dick said.

"I understand," Eddie mumbled.

"You okay, Eddie?" Duba asked. "You look a little pale."

"I'm okay. It's about that time is all. I get this way when I'm nervous. I'm okay. That bum…"

"There's nothing to be nervous about, Eddie," Dick said. "We have it under control. We're going to get your money. We've done this before. What can we do to set you at ease? And give you confidence that we'll come through for you?"

"What did you paratroopers do for nerves?" Duba asked.

"A lot of us drank or smoked," Eddie said. "I didn't smoke."

Dick turned and reached into his pocket. He pulled out a five-dollar bill.

"Go ahead, get yourself one," Dick said.

"One?" Eddie asked, looking confused.

"You said you could use a drink to calm your nerves," Dick said. "So, get one."

"Thanks," Eddie said.

"But no driving my car after you had a drink."

"I'll get a pint and wait until we get back to the plane," Eddie said.

"One drink," Dick said. "But you and Randy be at Myrtie's tonight for supper."

CHAPTER 18

THE SETUP

Ole Charlie here rose up on a signpost, watching Dick push Alice's wheelchair through the mysterious alleys of the state fair, each of them taking it all in. They turned into the Midway, making their way with an ease of slow, not wanting to draw attention. The wheelchair stopped at one tent, maybe fifteen feet away from the pickpocket.

Dick turned about, as if he was watching the Midway fun. The "Ring the Bell" challenge, where farmers and city folk alike stood in line to slam the oversized wooden sledge mallet to try to ring the bell and win a kewpie doll or a pocket comb, impressing their sweethearts.

Allowing Dick and Alice the time to get ahead of them, Conway, Duba, and Dwyer made their way through the front gate and then split up. They spaced themselves thirty feet apart and were careful to stay a distance from Alice's wheelchair. Conway took up a post listening to the talker for the girlie show. Dwyer stopped at the shooting gallery, stacking up quarters, and Duba stood in the line for the baseball throw at the wooden milk bottles.

Ole Charlie here moved and got my best, watchful advantage of the whole Midway, sitting on top of the merry-go-round, enjoying the sounds.

"Slam! Ding…"

"Slam! Ding…"

"Hurry, hurry, hurry! He's part man. He's part alligator. Come see the illusion…"

Alice turned her head about, taking in the Midway's sights and sounds before locking her eyes on the pickpocket, hoping he would sense that she was watching him.

It was fifteen minutes when the water witchery man, Marty, finally strutted up the Midway in his straw hat and the sign hanging from his neck.

"Water! Water!" Marty sang out. "Who needs water?"

He'd zig and he'd zag through the crowd, pretending he was searching out farmers who needed water wells.

"Why wait for a rain barrel to fill up when you don't have to, folks?" he preached. "Don't waste another planting. If water is what you need, it's Jedidiah and my magic stick here that will find water on your farm."

Marty would turn around, catch people's eyes.

"My magic stick never fails. Now who needs water on their farm? Water, anyone? I find water in a day or you get your money back—every penny."

He walked over to a man in a business suit.

"What's fifty bucks compared to a field of corn, mister?"

With a watchful eye, Alice waited like a crouched panther for the pickpocket to notice Marty, maybe size him up as a mark.

In time the pickpocket caught her eye. He had moved about the crowd, lifting a wallet or two, looked over at her twice, as if he were nervous about her watching him. Alice reached over her shoulder and tapped Dick's hand, signalling him.

"He's such a crumb, that guy," she said. "Let's get him."

"Are you ready?" Dick asked.

"I'm as ready as I'll ever be. Push me in closer, but keep me toward the middle of the Midway."

"Here goes," Dick said.

"That'll keep me away from prying ears. Close to the tents somebody might recognize me."

As Dick pushed, Alice lifted a large purse from under her lap blanket. She figured it might be a good lure. It was as large as Eddie's valise.

The pickpocket was a spiff. He had a shine on his shoes, a starched collar and a fresh carnation in his lapel.

"That's' an expensive tie he's wearing," Alice whispered to Dick. "Get me in closer."

"I wonder if he's Vichy French today or a Brit?" Dick asked.

"By the looks of his beret, could be either," Alice said.

When the pickpocket first looked over at Alice, he locked his eyes on her purse.

"We'll know soon enough," Alice said.

She was patient, waiting to catch his eye again.

He looked at her.

She jerked her head twice, motioning him over. Pickpocket winced and looked behind, as though he wasn't certain if she was signalling him or someone nearby. Again, she jerked her head twice. She rolled her eyes impatiently, raised a hand and wiggled her finger in a "come here, I want to talk," gesture.

It finally worked. He started toward the wheelchair.

Seeing him coming, Dick pretended not to notice and turned to look around the Midway like a tourist, at the same time getting a fix on where the chess players in this game were— Conway, Duba, and Dwyer. And Marty, of course.

"I'm sorry, but were you motioning to me, milady?" the pickpocket asked.

Alice leaned her head back, looked up at Dick.

"Get lost," she said. "I have business."

Dick stepped away from the chair and walked over by the bell ring game.

"Milady, I'm a guest in your country, spreading the word of the Sherlock Holmes Players."

"You are, are you?" Alice asked.

142

"We're bringing a bit of London to the American stage, tomorrow in the town of New Woodstock. May I interest you in free tickets for you and your mates? Free—it's such a demeaning term of value, isn't it, mum?"

"Nothin's free," Alice mumbled.

"We're papering the house; ticket sales for the first performance have been a tad dozy. Papering the house means—"

"Save it," Alice barked.

"There'll be two perfor—huh?"

"I have a proposition to make," Alice said.

"Why, ma'am I'm a simple thespian."

"Yeah, right," Alice said.

"Actually, I play Sherlock…"

"Put a sock in it, pal," Alice growled.

"Excuse me?"

"I didn't catch them all. You're pretty quick. But I did see a few. What'd you make picking those pockets? A few bucks? How many wallets did you get?"

"I must be going. Nice to have met you," the pickpocket scowled.

"You haven't met me, and you only wish you knew me. But I know you. Boy, do I know you."

"I beg your pardon."

"Beg all you want."

"Who are you?" the pickpocket asked.

"If I didn't think you were good enough, I wouldn't waste my breath," Alice said. "How'd you like to make some real money?"

"Excuse me?"

"I mean some real money, not this ten- and twenty-dollar stuff."

"Lady, are ye a copper?"

"Last chance, sailor. You want to make thousands or just twenties? It's time to stop flapping your gums and make a decision or I'm going, going, gone."

Pickpocket knelt next to the wheelchair.

143

"Talk to me, milady. How do you yanks say it? It's your quid?"

"It's your nickel," Alice said.

"I'm listening."

Alice caught Dick's eye and signalled him to come back and stand guard behind the chair. She didn't open her purse until Dick was there. She unsnapped the purse, reached in and took out five crisp, new twenty-dollar bills.

"See this?" she asked.

"I do indeed, milady," the pickpocket said.

"Pick a mark," Alice said.

"Excuse me?" the pickpocket asked.

"Over by that tent, over there, the shooting gallery," Alice said. "Pick a mark."

"I'll play your daffy game. Okay, the young couple. He's shooting the rifle, she's holding kewpie dolls," the pickpocket said.

The pickpocket didn't point to Dwyer.

"Nah, they're too much in love, way too young," Alice said.

"I beg your pardon," the pickpocket said. "I think that chap looks prime."

"He's probably still in college waiting tables at a neighbourhood bar—and they're broke," Alice said.

"How can you tell, mum?"

"She already has kewpie dolls and cotton candy. He's spending the last of his money," Alice said.

"You're absolutely right," the pickpocket said. "My, but you are smashing, mum. How about the fellow in overalls next to them? With the reddish hair?"

"Perfect choice," Alice said.

It was Dwyer.

"He probably still has the down-payment money his daddy gave him this morning to put on the new tractor in the farm equipment pavilion."

"And this means what, exactly?" the pickpocket asked.

144

Dick knew it was time. He watched until Dwyer looked around at him, catching his eye. Dick turned his head to the right and then to the left, indicating he had no cigarette over his ear. The signal was in. Dwyer turned his head away.

"Take these twenties over there and see if the redhead has a bigger bill," Alice said.

"Let me understand this," the pickpocket said. "You're telling me to take five twenty-dollar bills and go get it changed into two fifties or a single one-hundred-dollar bill?"

"Yes, go!"

"Am I missing something?"

"Let's just say it'll show me I can trust you, sailor. Then let's say it'll be your ticket to making a couple of thousand today, if you're smart. And that's in Yankee dollars."

"Well, these are numbers I clearly understand," the pickpocket said.

"I do talk pretty clear, don't I, sailor?"

"You certainly do, mum, and after we sort through this, we'll have a proper introduction."

"You don't like sailor, sailor?"

"I detest the sea, mum."

Alice handed him the twenties. He stood up, brushed off the knees of his trousers, straightened the knot in his tie and worked his way through the crowd to the rifle range. At first, he feigned walking past Dwyer, then turned as though on a spur of the moment and began speaking to him. He pointed to the girlie-girlie tent and reached in his pocket and pulled out the twenties, holding them in front of Dwyer. Dwyer nodded his head yes, reached in his pocket, handed the pickpocket a tattered, hundred-dollar bill and took the twenties. Not knowing if he was feeling a sense of accomplishment or a sense of confusion, the pickpocket walked back to the wheelchair. He knelt and handed Alice the hundred-dollar bill.

About that time, Alice did something causing Dick to near spit up. She handed the hundred-dollar bill back to the pickpocket.

"Keep this. You earned it," Alice said.

Dick's eyes got as big as cucumber slices. He bit his lower lip and hoped he was dreaming. Giving Big Mike's, Mike Shea's or Doc Webb's money away was not a part of the plan.

"This is a hundred American dollars, milady. Why are you giving it to me?"

"You earned it, sailor, and it didn't cost me a nickel."

"I'm sorry, but not having my morning tea, I thought I heard you say that giving away one hundred dollars didn't cost you anything."

"That's what I said, sailor."

"Did I get that right?"

"Mine wasn't real. That farmer made you one hundred dollars, and it didn't cost you or me anything."

"What are you saying?"

"The money you gave him for his hundred-dollar bill was counterfeit."

His mouth dropped. The pickpocket believed her. He believed the supposed real money was counterfeit, just as Dick and Duba said he would—because Alice said it was.

"Lady," the pickpocket said. "Are you sure you're not a copper?"

"Go ahead, try it again, sailor. Pick a mark."

"Let me see. Farmers have the money, you say?" the pickpocket asked.

"They're here to buy new farm equipment," Alice said.

"Only makes sense, now doesn't it, this being an agricultural exhibition. I say…"

"How about that tall gentleman over there by that cage?"

"The cricket cage?" the pickpocket asked.

"It's a baseball cage where they toss baseballs to hit bottles," Alice said.

"Precisely, that's it."

"Go over and see if he'll change these twenties."

Alice handed pickpocket five more brand new twenties.

Pickpocket took the money and stood up. He gave a thought to disappearing. After all, the wheelchair lady had picked this mark. It was probably a setup, he thought. He paused at first, and then he decided to at least try and walked toward the baseball cage.

Dick caught Duba's eye and turned his head both ways, signalling there was no cigarette. The mark was set. Pickpocket worked his way over, walked by him and turned back, inquiring if he could make change. Duba said no, he couldn't. Pickpocket shrugged his shoulders and walked back to the wheelchair.

"He didn't have more than a twenty on him," the pickpocket said.

Now he was a believer, but Alice didn't leave anything to chance. She'd try again.

"Okay, last time, or I'm out of here, sailor," Alice said. "Make it good. Now what sorts of gents want to hide their folding money, hide it the best?"

"Those who are afraid of temptation and the pocket lifters," the pickpocket said.

"Exactly," Alice said. "See the two farmers over there by the girlie show?"

"I do," the pickpocket said.

"The one on the left, doesn't he have a crease on his back pocket, probably a wallet with a lot of money in it? Take this and see if he wants to change small bills for it."

Alice handed pickpocket two crisp new hundred-dollar bills. Pickpocket looked at the two bills. He could take them and run and be ahead three hundred Yankee dollars. But his greed kicked in.

"Wish me god speed," he said.

Dick placed a cigarette over his ear, turned and watched for Conway to notice it while pickpocket was straightening his beret and tie. Conway did. The signal was in.

Pickpocket stood and walked over to the gathering in front of the girlie show. As the crowd shuffled, he made his way over, sidling up to Conway. Casually he opened his wallet and lifted out the hundred-dollar bills. He began folding them small as though he wanted to go see the girlie show but didn't want to risk losing them. He pretended he wanted to hide the two hundred-dollar bills. Conway took notice.

"Want to trade those?" Conway asked.

"Pardon me?" the pickpocket asked.

"I want to get rid of some tens and twenties. Want to trade my small bills for your hundreds?"

"Perfect solution," the pickpocket said. "Why is it we men worry about losing our big bills but not smaller ones?"

"Beats me, friend," Conway said.

They made the trade and the pickpocket worked his way back to the wheelchair.

"This is amazing," the pickpocket said. "I never dreamed it would be so easy. The bills you have are brilliantly done."

"Nothing but the best," Alice said. "They come in by boat from Canada. You want some of them, sailor? Beats—how'd you call it—lifting pockets?"

"I certainly do, if the price is right, I certainly do."

Pickpocket handed the two hundred dollars to Alice.

"Keep it," she said.

Dick was about to have a heart attack. He took the cigarette from his ear and lit it, choking on his first drag.

"Can you come up with a thousand US?" Alice asked.

The pickpocket looked at the three hundred he had just made, knew about seven hundred he had stolen and looked over at Alice.

"I can, absolutely," he said.

Alice leaned her head back, caught Dick's eye.

"Get lost."

Just as well, Dick had to go find a toilet where he could puke, cry or whatever was going to be his reaction to this fourth-grade school teacher giving a known criminal, a thief, a crook, three hundred real US dollars that didn't belong to any of them.

"A thousand greenbacks will get you five thousand in assorted bills."

"My, my," the pickpocket said, adjusting the knot in his tie.

"There's a catch," Alice said.

"I'm certain there would be," the pickpocket said.

"You can only use five hundred of it here in Syracuse. Take the rest with you, out of town, back to England, but not here. We don't want locals to get wise and close in."

149

"Makes good sense," the pickpocket said. "Perfect sense, indeed."

By this time Dick had reappeared. Alice caught his eye and flagged him over to the wheelchair.

"Sailor, it's time you meet Jedidiah," Alice said.

"Jedidiah?" the pickpocket asked.

"He's the link to the funny money. I'll arrange it. Go get me a hot dog and lemonade, will you?" Alice handed him ten dollars.

"Oh, no," the pickpocket said. "My treat."

Pickpocket walked to a hot dog tent and stood in line, smiling, thinking of his soon-to-be riches.

Without moving his lips and risking drawing notice, Dick pleaded.

"Are you crazy, Alice? Are you nuts? You just gave a crook three hundred real bucks that, I might remind you, doesn't belong to us."

"We'll get it back tonight," Alice said. "Don't worry."

"Want to clue me in as to how?" Dick asked, his heart palpitating.

"He's going to give Marty a thousand bucks tonight, right?"

"Well, yes, it looks like it," Dick said.

"So there. That'll be Big Mike's, Mike Shea's and Doc Webb's money, plus we get Eddie's seven hundred back."

"Oh," Dick said, somewhat relieved. "But Eddie only lost six hundred forty."

"Well, we'll let Sheriff Todd worry about the change."

By this time the pickpocket returned with hot dogs and lemonades for them.

"I love American hot dogs. They're such a tasty delight with all the garnishments."

"Let's eat first, and then I'll get you to Jedidiah so you can talk business."

"And you get?" the pickpocket asked.

"I get a finder's fee. Jedidiah takes care of me, don't worry."

"Such a nice arrangement," the pickpocket said.

The three of them—a fourth-grade teacher in disguise, a sixteen-year-old who dreamed up this SOS, and a pickpocketing actor from Liverpool—standing together in the early afternoon sun, enjoying hot dogs and lemonade. The smells of cotton candy and salt water taffy wafted through the air, the milling crowds growing with the day.

The bait was set, the lure had worked. Now it was time for the big show—time to spring the trap. While waiting for Marty to come up through the Midway again they listened to the carny noises and sounds—bells ringing, clickers clicking, talkers promising their crowd the moon, anything they would believe. They enjoyed it. After all, it was the New York State Fair.

The pickpocket was a pleasant enough sort. An interesting bloke, as he would say. He happened to be a no-account crook is all, and had to be stopped. Dick looked at his watch. Marty was only going to walk through putting on his show every hour on the hour. They had time. Pickpocket bought them another round of hot dogs and lemonade.

CHAPTER 19

WATER WITCHERY

"That's Delphi Falls Road up ahead," Randy said. "You'll want to turn left on it."

Eddie pointed toward the right.

"Is that a store over there?"

"That's Hastings, yup," Randy said.

"I ought to get my girls something before I take off to Binghamton tomorrow."

"Why don't we go to the plane first and put the gas in it?" Randy asked. "We'll bring the cans back, and you can get a look around the store then."

"Sounds good," Eddie said.

"If you don't see anything you like, we'll try Shea's corner. They have a lot of stuff. Dick won't mind your using the car for that," Randy said.

He parked the car on the shoulder of the road, and the two walked through the field to the plane. With Randy on one side and Eddie on the other, they lifted the tarpaulin, folded it like a bed sheet and put it on the ground by the fence. Eddie pulled the unopened pint of whiskey from his pocket and set it in the back cockpit of the plane. Randy held the funnel while Eddie poured the gasoline, emptying the cans.

"This'll get me to Binghamton," Eddie said.

"Let's take the cans to Hastings, and you can look for something for your kids," Randy said.

"Hold on a second," Eddie said. "Let me check something out."

Eddie climbed into the back cockpit. He picked up the two-way radio microphone knob.

"What is that telephone operator's name again?"

"Myrtie," Randy said.

Eddie pushed his thumb down on the button. With his other hand he kept turning the dial on the two-way radio receiver, listening for sound.

"Calling Myrtie. This is Flying Eddie, calling Myrtie. Come in, Myrtie," he spoke clearly into the microphone. He released the button and waited.

There was hissing, whistling, and buzzing as he turned the tuning dial.

"Myrtie, come in. Calling Myrtie. Come in, Myrtie."

He fiddled and spoke, turned the knob and tried again.

"Myrtie, come in. This is Flying Eddie calling Myrtie. Come in, Myrtie."

Finally, it happened.

"Myrtie here…come in, Flying Eddie. Over."

"Roger that, Myrtie, this is Flying Eddie and Randy calling from my plane down here at the Delphi Falls, come in…"

"You're breaking up, Flying Eddie, breaking up bad. Where are you flying?" Myrtie squawked.

"I'm on the ground at the Delphi Falls, Myrtie," Eddie said. "Can you hear me? Over."

"I hear scratching—can make out some, Eddie. Sheriff Hood said you might test. He'll be here at seven…come back…"

"Roger, Myrtie…just checking the system…We'll be here waiting to hear from you from seven on…"

"Roger," Myrtie said.

"If it breaks up then, we'll take her up for better reception," Eddie shouted. "Come back."

"I'll tell Sheriff Hood," Myrtie said.

153

"Over and out," Eddie said. He hung the microphone on the hook on the dash of the cockpit.

Randy's eyes were as big as quarters.

"This hill next to us is going to be a problem," Eddie said.

"It goes all the way back to the falls," Randy said. "It's all shale cliff on the other side of it by the creek."

"The rock is blocking the radio antenna's reception," Eddie said.

"When you're flying with the open cockpit and all, how can you hear the radio?" Randy asked.

"With these," Eddie said.

He picked up earphones with a microphone attached from the floor. "You wear these and plug this knob into the two-way."

"Wow," was about all Randy had to offer.

"Let's take the gas cans back," Eddie said. "Help me get them in the trunk."

"What then?" Randy asked. "We have all afternoon to kill."

"After we get back, we'll charge the battery of the plane so the two-way will be strong," Eddie said.

"How do we do that?"

"We'll chock the wheels of the plane, so she won't roll anywhere, and we'll start her up. You can sit in the cockpit fifteen minutes while the battery charges."

"I can?" Randy beamed.

"While we're waiting on that, I'll walk to Farmer Parker's and see if he needs me for a chore."

Randy grinned from ear to ear.

"I'll come back and turn it off when it's time. Just don't touch any knobs or switches while it's running."

Randy beamed at the thought of him being trusted to sit behind the stick of an honest-to-goodness 1941 single engine biplane while its motor revved and its propeller spun. Life could never get better than this for a lad, he was likely thinking. They gathered the gasoline cans and headed to the car.

154

"While I sit in it, you know, when it's idling, can I put on the helmet and earphones?" Randy asked.

"Put on the goggles, too. Just don't touch any switches or buttons."

Meanwhile back on the Midway at the New York State Fair, Marty, the water witchery master was about to go into his act again. He had timed it so he would make one quick walk through the Midway on the hour until the trap was set. The last thing he wanted was someone who needed water.

Alice caught Marty's eye from four tents away. He was hanging the sign on his neck looking around the crowd for her or Dick. When they connected, Alice reached behind and tapped Dick's hand to signal Marty. He was to clue Marty that they'd identified the pickpocket mark and were ready to begin their charade. Dick put a cigarette over each ear and turned about. Marty saw the cigarettes, tipped his straw hat and nodded. The signal was in. With that, Dick took one of the cigarettes from an ear and lit it.

"Sailor," Alice said. "You ready to make the connection?"

"I am, milady," the pickpocket said, wiping mustard from his chin.

"You'd better be able to come up with the money, or there'll be a big mess," Alice said.

"I have it, I assure you, mum. I'll have more than a thousand dollars American in my bag at the playhouse. I will not let you down. Your commission is safe."

Marty pranced his way past the rifle range.

"Water! Water!" Marty bellowed. "Water on your farm!"

He slowed his walk, waiting for the fish to bite.

"There he is," Alice said. "Over there with the sign."

"The chap and his water-witchery, mum?" the pickpocket asked.

"That's him," Alice said.

"Why that chap has been strolling through all day. Are you certain?"

"Why wait for rain, when you don't have to, folks," Marty preached. "Don't waste another planting—if water is what you want, Jedidiah and my magic stick is what you need. A water well is what you'll get. My stick never fails to find water…"

"That's his front here at the fair," Alice said. "But he actually can find water for farmers. He knows how."

"I wouldn't have ever…" the pickpocket started.

"He's the source for what you want. Go do your business, sailor. Make it good."

The pickpocket straightened his tie and walked over to Marty.

"Who needs water on the farm?" Marty barked. "Water anyone?"

The pickpocket tapped Marty's arm.

"Sir, I need to ask you something," the pickpocket whispered.

"The answer is yes, I can find water anywhere," Marty said.

"But I—" the pickpocket started.

"I find water in a day or you get your money back. What's fifty bucks compared to the cost of planting a field of corn, mister?"

"As a matter of curiosity, how are you able to find water using a stick, if I may ask?" the pickpocket asked.

"It's a branch from a tree that bears a fruit with seeds in it. Fruit needs water to grow. Nature points the branch to water the same way sunflower turn to the sun. This twig will find water as far as twenty feet down."

"Simply smashing," the pickpocket said.

Marty began to turn away.

"I have a thousand, how you say, greenbacks, to spend if you have any of the other goods I've been told of," the pickpocket said.

"Beat it, friend. I'm trying to earn an honest living here, nothing more. Water! Who needs water on the farm?"

The pickpocket pulled the hundred-dollar bills from his pocket. He fanned them out. Marty leaned and spoke from the side of his jaw.

"That's a little short, fella. Take a hike!" Marty barked in a loud raspy whisper. "Water, who needs water, folks?"

"I've got another seven hundred at the playhouse in New Woodstock. I promise I have it all. A thousand, I believe I was told."

"I don't see the thousand," Marty said.

"Milady over there will vouch for me. We can make an exchange tomorrow."

"If we do anything, it'll be tonight," Marty said.

"I have to be in a rehearsal all afternoon. I'm in the play."

"Over in that wheelchair?"

"That's her."

"You have all the money?" Marty asked.

"Can you show me some identity?" the pickpocket asked. "How do I know you're not a copper?"

Marty started, thought about the card he got at the Cortland carnival and reached deep in his pocket and pulled out the card for Jedidiah and his séance gatherings.

"Why that card's not about water, it says séances. Say, what gives, Gov?"

Marty gulped.

"See that name?"

"I see it," the pickpocket said.

"It's Jedidiah—that's me. I find water when ground isn't frozen. I do séances when it is. Have to make a living somehow."

Beads of sweat were sparkling Marty's freckles, but he took charge again.

"You have the money or not, fella?"

"Every greenback, my good man."

"Do you know the Lincklaen House hotel?

157

"Yes, in fact, I do, Mate. We're staying there, in Cazenovia. It's a short jaunt from our playhouse in a New Woodstock school theater."

Marty leaned in. "Listen up."

"I'm listening."

"There's a telephone closet in the lobby of that hotel."

"I know the one," the pickpocket said.

"Get in it before eight o'clock tonight and wait for a ring."

"I was going to work the Midway until nine, be at the hotel about ten. Might we do this tomorrow?"

"See ya'," Marty snorted, turning away.

"No wait, I'll be there," the pickpocket said. "I'll be there, precisely at eight o'clock."

"That's better," Marty growled.

"Tonight, it is then, in the phone closet."

"Now you're getting smart," Marty said. "When it rings, answer it. Somebody will ask for a code."

"A code, I understand," the pickpocket said.

"The code you give 'em is, Mary had a little lamb…"

"Mary had a little lamb?!" The pickpocket groaned in disbelief.

"Get it right, or the deal's off," Marty said.

"I will, I will. Mary had a little lamb. I've got it."

"Not so loud."

"Sorry."

"And you'd better have the cash on you when you get there."

"Might'n I get some of it from you now?"

"Do you see any bags on me?"

"Well that small one, but…"

"See any trunks I'm dragging around behind me? Do you?"

"Sorry, I didn't mean…"

"Be in the telephone closet at eight o'clock, answer the phone, give the code. You'll get a code word back and directions where to pick it up. How simple is that?"

"Will it be far from the hotel?" I don't have an auto, you see."

"Figure it out. Just answer the telephone and give your code. By the way, what's your name?"

The pickpocket looked about the Midway.

"Call me Sherlock Holmes, my good man," he said. "We'll do business tonight and you come as my guest to see us perform tomorrow. Sherlock Holmes is at your service, sir."

"Just be there with the money."

"I suppose I might hail a taxi."

"Not my problem. You'd better have all the money, or you'll walk away empty-handed, and that means without the three hundred in your pocket. I'll call it a fine for wasting my time. Lincklaen House lobby telephone closet at eight. Now get lost before we get spotted."

The pickpocket watched Marty walk away, up the Midway.

He folded the bills, put them in his pocket and turned to go talk with wheelchair milady. He looked at the spot where he had left her and her helper (Dick). They were gone. He stepped back into the middle of the Midway and looked for them in front of tents, each attraction. Wheelchair lady had disappeared. Pickpocket was okay with that. He figured he was up three hundred American, if nothing came down. He had nothing to lose. He turned about again to watch the water witchery gentlemen. Marty had disappeared as well—completely out of sight. The pickpocket had some time before his fellow actor's ride to the Lincklaen House in Cazenovia came. He wedged himself into a crowd at the girlie show tent and lifted some unsuspecting farmers' pockets along the way.

As Marty stepped through the exit columns of the state fair's entrance, Duba jumped from behind one.

"Boo!" he barked.

"Where's Conway?" Marty asked.

"Randy and Eddie went to Delphi Falls. Conway is taking Alice home for a nap."

"Conway was supposed to get me to Cazenovia," Marty said.

159

"Alice was worn out from being keyed up all night. She said she needed to soak in a tub and nap after being in the sun all day."

"She was perfect," Marty said. "That pickpocket bought her story, hook, line, and sinker."

"He'll never know what hit him," Duba said. "I'm driving you to Cazenovia."

"Okay."

"Dick and Dwyer are taking the lot of them—Randy, Barber, and Holbrook—over to Myrtie's to wait for Sheriff Hood. Myrtie is making supper."

"I have to get a copy of the map to the camp," Marty said.

"Tall Jerry is already setting up your camp, with the fire and all. He went there with Farmer Parker and Mr. Ossant when they took the team of horses and wagon in. He stayed there."

"I need to use a telephone."

"I'm taking you to the Lincklaen House to get your map first," Duba said. "You can use the phone there."

"Now," Marty barked.

"Why now?" Duba asked.

"I've gotta' tell Myrtie what time to call the hotel. You have a nickel for the telephone?" Marty asked.

Duba walked Marty to a telephone booth and handed him two nickels. Marty dropped in a coin and dialed "O."

"Operator. How may I assist you please?"

"Operator, I need the operator in New Woodstock," Marty said. "Can you connect me?"

"One moment, puleeeze…"

"How much do I put in, ma'am?"

"It's an operator exchange call, sir."

"How much?"

"There's no charge."

"It's free?"

"There is no charge for an operator exchange call, sir."

"Oh, I see. Thank you."

"Operator, how may I help you?"

"Hello?

"This is the operator."

"Hello. Myrtie, this is Marty."

"Marty, are you coming for supper?"

"I can't, I'll be at the camp."

"Be careful, Marty."

"Myrtie, I'm supposed to give you the time you're to call the telephone closet at the Lincklaen House."

"Oh, that's right."

"Call it at eight o'clock, Myrtie. Let it ring until he answers it."

"I most certainly will," Myrtie said. "What do I tell him?"

"You ask for his code. He'll say the code. It's 'Mary had a little lamb.'"

Myrtie howled through the phone.

"I know, I know. It sounds stupid. It's all my brain could come up with. I was nervous thinking the guy might get wise and pull a knife or gun or something."

"It's perfect, sweetie. Just perfect," Myrtie said. "Mary had a little lamb."

"Okay," Marty said. "When he answers with that code, tell him to ask the front desk for the envelope for Sherlock Holmes. There's one there waiting for him. It will have a map to the hideout where he pays for and picks up the goods."

"Clever," Myrtie said.

"Tell him when he gets to the hideout his code word is going to be 'séance.'"

"Séance?" Myrtie asked.

"Yes. Tell him he has to say, 'I'm here for the séance' before he'll be let in the camp."

"My, what fun," Myrtie said. "I have all of this written down, so don't worry about a thing, honey. Be careful tonight."

"Thanks, Myrtie."

"Anything else?" Myrtie asked.

"Oh, tell Sheriff Hood his envelope with a copy of the map to the camp is at the hotel lobby desk."

"He'll need that map for sure," Myrtie said.

Tell him it's marked for him as 'Messenger.' He'll need it to make the arrest. Tell him not to lose it. No one knows where the camp is without that map. I don't even know where it is until I get my copy."

"I'll be certain to tell him," Myrtie said. "My, but you've thought of every detail."

As Marty hung up, Duba pulled around in his pickup and waited for him to climb in. They headed off to Cazenovia to get Marty's copy of the map and then to his secret camp hideout.

"Duba, something's come up," Marty said.

"Like what?" Duba asked.

"I need your help," Marty said, as they pulled into Cazenovia.

"Did you just think about it now?" Duba asked.

"The pickpocket said he didn't have a ride to the camp."

"How's he getting to the Lincklaen House?"

"He stays there. The actors drive him. We don't want any of the actors driving him to the campsite."

"That won't work, you're right." Duba said.

"I have an idea," Marty said.

"Shoot," Duba barked.

"Can you make a sign that says TAXI and put it on the door of your truck?"

"Huh?" Duba asked.

"The pickpocket doesn't have wheels. If you're parked in front of the Lincklaen House pretending to be a taxi, you could watch for him and be the one to give him a ride to wherever my camp is."

"Why me?"

"You have a pickup, and after I get my copy of the map and you take me to the camp, you'll be the only one who will know how to get there…"

"I get it, I get it," Duba said. "What time?"

"You have to be early. Myrtie is going to call him at eight o'clock, and he'll be ready to go then."

"I'll be there early."

"After Sheriff Hood gets the map he'll go to the camp and hide in the wagon. Tall Jerry is already there. You're the only one not doing anything."

"I see a problem," Duba said.

"What's that?"

"What if a state trooper or deputy stops and asks what I'm doing with a taxi sign on my truck sitting in front of the hotel?"

"Then don't be sitting in front of the hotel until eight o'clock. This ain't New York City, for crying out loud. Nobody in Cazenovia is going to pay any attention to a sign on the door of an old truck."

"Probably not," Duba said.

"Park somewhere else and kill time listening to the radio."

"Can't."

"Can't what?"

"Can't listen to my radio."

"Huh?"

"No antenna. Can't tune in my radio with no antenna."

The pickup pulled up to the hotel. Marty got out, ran in and got his copy of the map. Two maps were left there, one for Sheriff Todd Hood (in the envelope marked 'Messenger') and the other for the pickpocket marked 'Sherlock Holmes.' Duba and Marty studied the map, and Duba drove down Albany Street and then over to Cherry Valley and down it to Pompey Hollow Road. Duba pulled onto the shoulder at the corner where he dropped Marty off to find his camp on foot.

"It's maybe a hundred yards over on Pompey Hollow Road," Duba said. "Not too far."

"There's a dirt path up to it somewhere near about. From the map it looks like it may be a hundred yards in," Marty said.

"Look for the path near spinster Nettie's place and turn in there, I'm thinking," Duba said.

"It won't take me long," Marty said.

"There's a car path goes in quite a way," Duba said. "Mostly apple trees all about, some maple."

"How do you know all this?" Marty asked. "Car path and apple trees?"

"Us guys would take girls in there to neck."

"I swear, is that all you and Dick ever think about, kissing and girls?"

"Pretty much," Duba said.

"Well, if you know the place, drop me off there."

"They said I'm not to take you in, in case we're being followed and watched. You have to hike it. Good luck."

Duba headed home near Shea's corner to paint a TAXI sign and get food provisions for his vigil later. It could be a long night, and he wanted to be prepared. As he painted the sign, he devoured two peanut butter and jelly sandwiches, one cheese and mayonnaise sandwich, a dill pickle, and a quart of milk. He paper-sacked some vittles for later.

Returning to Cazenovia, he edged just up the street from the Lincklaen House entrance and parked in front of the movie house. He sat there a full forty-five minutes looking at the movie posters, waiting in silence before he lit his last cigarette. Smoking that one, he leaned over and checked his glove box for another pack. Then he sat some more.

His plan was to turn the truck around just before eight o'clock and pull it down and park it in front of the hotel and attach his taxi sign so it would be clearly visible for the pickpocket when he stepped out of the hotel. Until then, being quiet and incognito was his plan.

It was during those quiet moments of incognito that it happened. A thought came to Duba. It was a vision, like a mirage that happens after a body walks through a desert too long without water or sits too long in a pickup staring at movie posters without a radio antenna with two house flies. He was inspired. He bolted into the Lincklaen House and right up to the lobby desk clerk.

"Do you have an envelope for 'Messenger?'" he asked.

The desk clerk in her starched white blouse and collar picked the envelope marked 'Messenger' from a basket labelled 'Important Papers.'

"This note says Messenger will be picking this up at seven o'clock, sir. It's only six o'clock. Are you Messenger?" the lady asked.

"I'm the courier to get it to 'Messenger,' ma'am."

Duba's brain likened that courier was to 'Messenger' as general might be to sergeant.

She handed him the envelope.

"Thank you, sir," she said.

"Thank you, lady," Duba said.

He was going to wait in his pickup and be a hero by personally handing the envelope to Sheriff Hood the second he drove up at seven o'clock. After all, Sheriff Hood was a busy man.

Duba climbed back into his pickup and adjusted his rear view mirror and side mirror so he would see the reflection of Sheriff Hood's vehicle when it turned onto the street from Albany Street and pulled in front of the hotel.

A sigh came over him for his stealth and cunning. As a reward he reached into the sack, beating the two houseflies to half the chicken salad on white. Then half the egg salad sandwich with black olive slices. The bag of Wise potato chips kept his hands busy. The lad believed the noise of their crunch would keep him alert. He washed it down with one of his two bottles of Nehi orange soda pop, conserving one to go with the other two sandwich halves.

He turned about and tried several positions before he settled on one resting his head against the back window of his pickup. He fixed his eyes on the side mirror, pinpointing the exact spot where Sheriff Hood's car would be driving behind him.

All the efficiency only made his leg cramp and him hungry. He ate the rest of the sandwiches and finished off his last Nehi. He could now stretch the cramped leg up on the dashboard.

All in all, it was quite a day.

Alice and Marty outdid themselves with performances on the Midway. Alice would have stories to tell. Randy and Eddie got the battery charged on the biplane and found Raggedy Ann dolls for Eddie's two little girls at Shea's.

Marty found the campsite. He and Jerry had wood stacked, a campfire ablaze and were stirring some eggs and diced Spam in a skillet, looking for some pepper, an onion, and coffee grounds.

Holbrook, Randy, Bases, and Barber with combed hair, fingernails cleaned, were dropped off at Myrtie's in New Woodstock by Randy's pop, and waited as proper houseguests for supper.

Myrtie was dashing about her second-story flat in New Woodstock tending operator duties in her bedroom, keeping an eye out the window for Sheriff Hood, all while cooking supper in the kitchen.

Duba kept his vigil, staring through the pickup's side mirror, determined to impress the man he and Dick had differences of opinions with if Sheriff Hood would catch them speeding or drag racing.

Ole Charlie here, danced about, keeping an eye on them all.

As the evening wore on, Myrtie and the lads enjoyed a bottle of Pepsi, talking about the team Dick sent to the state fair. Holbrook and Randy were settin' on Myrtie's side-porch swing, pondering whether to split the Almond Joy candy bar first or the Mounds bar first after supper. Alice would be along whenever Conway picked her up. Dick and Dwyer were husking corn, feeling confident about the detail they had used in luring the pickpocket.

Duba was still at his post, sitting in his pickup, beaming a smile with a full stomach. A glaring setting sun reflected from the mirror in his eyes, rendering him mesmerized. While looking into the blinding sun his eyes started wriggling at first and then rolling and closing and crossing, then rolling again, his lids trying but failing to keep up with it all.

Sheriff Todd Hood was half a block from the hotel when he slowed his squad car in the bright setting sun. It was as he was driving past the library on Albany Street and starting his turn into the front of the Lincklaen House when Duba, with the sheriff's copy of the map resting on his lap, lost the battle of two Nehi soda pops, six sandwiches, and a setting sun, and dozed off to sleep.

It was right at seven, like clockwork, Sheriff Hood parked in front of the hotel door, ran in to get a map that wasn't there for him, returned to his car, scratched his head and drove off.

CHAPTER 20

WHO'S ON FIRST?

"Mrs Parker, Randy and I got the milking done," Eddie said.

"We appreciate you boys."

"The cows are in the pasture and the spreader's loaded."

"Fay needed this break. The ride to Albany with Mr. Ossant will do him good. Thank you for offering to do the milking for him."

"Randy here is a good teacher. I enjoyed learning," Eddie said. "We'll be going down to the plane now."

"I guess you'll be leaving us soon," Mrs. Parker said.

"I want to listen on the two-way radio for signals from Sheriff Hood."

"It's dusk, Eddie," Mrs. Parker said. "Why don't you boys let me feed you before you go to the plane. You'll need energy."

The two agreed, stepped over to the garden hose by the hen house and freshened up for an early supper.

Ole Charlie here set above the stove, watching the pork chops in the skillet, a perfect burnt edge to the fat.

"Eddie, I know you're leaving tomorrow," Mrs. Parker said. "We have some things we want you to take."

"You and Farmer Parker are way too kind, Mrs. Parker."

"Oh, they're not from us. We all chipped in. The packages will be here for you to take, but you have to promise to put them under your Christmas tree and no peeking."

"You have my word," Eddie said.

Mrs. Parker handed Eddie a plate of chops and a potato.

168

"I'll wager a big hug from your wife and two little girls in your arms will go a long way while you're figuring work for the winter— helping on a farm or something. There's always work on a farm."

"You're right."

"Turn to them first. Family will never let you down."

"Thank you. That's sound advice."

"Get some more potatoes and gravy, hon. Use that spoon."

"Mrs. Parker, I get the feeling you're trying to tell me something you haven't told me yet."

"One of you boys take the last chop."

"What are you thinking Mrs. Parker? I can take it."

"Eddie, they're trying their best to get your money back for you."

"I know. Mighty kind of them taking chances like this."

"But what if they don't?"

"Don't get the money back?"

"Yes."

"To be honest, Mrs. Parker, back of my head I never thought they could."

"So, let's say they aren't able to get your money."

"Mrs. Parker you won't tell Mary I said that, please."

"I won't dear, but what if they don't find your money?"

"Well then, Mrs. Parker, I'll get a good night's sleep in the straw loft, I'll wake early and have a nice breakfast, if I'm invited, that is. I'll thank my new friends for trying, and I'll crank up the plane and fly home."

Mrs. Parker had a gentle smile in her eye.

"You boys take the coffee percolator and our canteen cups to drink from. You can bring them back tonight," Mrs. Parker said.

Eddie and Randy stepped out and onto the back deck. The moon was full; the stars were twinkling down on budding lifetime friendships.

"Take the kerosene lantern," Mrs. Parker said. "It's full, and it'll outlast flashlight batteries."

She handed Eddie some kitchen stick matches. Randy held the lantern while Eddie lit it. They stepped off the porch and walked across the lawn and down toward the field where the plane was.

"That's a nice lady," Eddie said.

"Eddie, can you teach me how to fly sometime?"

"I'd be happy to, my friend. How about I give you a ride tomorrow before I head out, and, if you like it, I'll give you some lessons next year when I come up to the state fair?"

Randy beamed. He was holding the lantern up to look into Eddie's eyes to see if he looked sincere when they heard a crackling and popping sound through the quiet full moonlit night.

"Listen!" Eddie said.

The two halted.

"What is that?" Randy asked.

"Here it?" Eddie asked.

The crackling broke through the stillness of the night again, hissing and sputtering.

"Did you leave the two-way radio on?" Eddie asked.

"I think I did."

"Sounds like the radio," Eddie said.

"Charging the battery with the plane running, I turned the plane off like you told me, Eddie, but I forgot to turn the two-way radio off."

"Run," Eddie said. "I think someone's trying to call in."

Randy set the percolator and tin cups down by the side of the road. He grabbed the lantern and they ran through the field to the plane.

"Keep the lantern away from gas fumes," Eddie said.

HISS…POP…SCRATCH

"Sheriff Todd Hood calling…"

HISS… POP…

"Come in Eddie…"

CRACKLE… HISS.

Eddie jumped onto the wing of the plane and climbed into the rear cockpit, grabbing the microphone and pushing the button.

"This is Eddie, come in, Sheriff Hood…"

No answer.

"This is Eddie, come in, Sheriff Hood…"

There were scratching sounds.

No answer.

"We don't have a good connection," Eddie said.

"Did I break it?" Randy asked.

"It's this hill blocking the signal."

"So we won't be able to listen?" Randy asked.

"We won't have a good connection until we're in the air."

"Are we going up?" Randy asked.

"Randy, you have to run over to Farmer Parker's. Use their telephone and get Myrtie on the wire."

"Okay."

"See if Myrtie knows what Sheriff Hood wants. Ask her why he's calling. "

"Won't he be there with her?" Randy asked.

"If he is, you can ask him."

"Roger Wilko," Randy shouted.

He leaped from the plane's wing and ran like all get-out, grabbing up the lantern along the way.

Eddie cupped his hands and shouted. "See if Farmer Parker has a leather jacket or heavy coat you can wear. We might have to take her up. It gets mighty cold, especially at night."

Eddie stopped clicking the switch on the microphone. He didn't want to risk wearing out the battery.

Mary's dad drove up Cardner Road, let her out and drove off into the night. Seeing Eddie at the plane, she walked over.

"I delivered my papers early and was coming to see who was going to Myrtie's," Mary said. "You need help out here, Eddie?"

171

"You're a paper-girl too?" Eddie asked. "What other surprises are there about Mary?"

"That's about it, when I'm not selling popsicles from my cart summers in the hamlet, I deliver papers on Berry Road. What's up?"

It wasn't fifteen minutes when Randy came running back through the field. He was toting a sheepskin jacket and a pair of work gloves.

"He never got his map," Randy panted breathlessly. "He never got his map."

"Slow down. Take a deep breath," Eddie said.

"Were in big trouble," Randy panted.

"Who didn't get his map?" Eddie asked.

"The sheriff didn't get a map to the camp," Randy said.

"You mean they didn't draw a map?"

"They would have drawn a map, they promised."

"But the sheriff didn't get a copy of the map?" Eddie asked.

"There was no map for him at the Lincklaen House, so he doesn't know where the camp is."

"I saw Mr. Ossant take paper and envelopes just so he could draw maps when he and Farmer Parker got the wagon to wherever the camp was going to be," Mary said.

"Something happened to it," Eddie said.

"One envelope was supposed to be at the hotel waiting for Sheriff Hood," Mary said.

"There's been some kind of foul-up. There was no map there for him," Randy said.

"This could mean nobody knows where the camp is," Mary said.

"If nobody knows where the camp is, we'll never get your money, Eddie," Randy said.

"And if nobody can find the camp, Sheriff Hood can't make an arrest," Mary said.

"The problem is we don't even know where the camp is," Eddie said. "We can't tell anybody where it is."

"I was making salads and devilled eggs with Mrs. Parker when they left," Mary said. "All I know is Mr. Ossant was driving his car, following Farmer Parker and Tall Jerry driving the horses and wagon. They had the envelopes for the maps."

"Did they hint where they were going?" Eddie asked.

"No. It was a great looking wagon, it looked real. They never mentioned where they were taking it."

Eddie jumped off the wing.

"Randy, did the sheriff say anything else?"

"Like what?"

"Did he give you any ideas, any clues?"

"Yes!" Randy said. "He said to ask if you could find the camp with the biplane."

"He did?" Eddie asked.

"Yes."

"When were you going to tell me that?"

"Sorry, I forgot."

"That's smart," Mary said.

"I said I was sorry," Randy said.

"Not that, our finding the camp," Mary said.

"We could sure try," Eddie said.

"Sheriff said if you find the camp you could radio its location."

Eddie took off his leather flight jacket and handed it to Mary.

"Here, Mary, put this on."

"What?"

"You'll need it."

Mary took the flight jacket and put it on, rolling up the sleeves with a grin.

"When I tell you, jump into the front cockpit, both of you," Eddie said.

"Are we going to fly?" Randy asked.

"We're going to find us a campsite," Eddie shouted.

Randy and Mary started to climb on the wings.

"Have to pull the chocks away from the wheels," Eddie said. "I'll do it."

"Do you have to crank the propeller?" Randy asked.

"Yep, then I pull the chocks."

Mary was standing on the wing, leaning in over the side of the front cockpit.

"Grab the flashlight, Randy," Eddie said. "Neither of you touch anything unless I say, understood?"

"I understand," Randy said.

"I'm not touching anything," Mary said.

"This is so great," Randy said.

"Find my leather helmet and earphones. Take them into the front cockpit with you both."

"Where are they?" Randy asked.

"Look around. They'll be in the back cockpit somewhere, probably on the seat."

"I found them," Randy said.

"Take the goggles off them and give those to Mary. She'll need goggles. Randy, you wear the helmet and earphones."

"Gotcha," Randy said.

"Crawl into the front cockpit, both of you."

Randy grabbed the apparatus and did what he was told. Mary pulled the goggles on over her eyes. She took them off and tightened the straps and put them on again, tucking her hair back.

Eddie stepped on the wing to check some gauges. He paused to gather his thoughts. Randy flicked the flashlight on, inspecting the front cockpit where he and Mary were to sit, places they might be able to grab onto. The radio kept hissing.

"Are you both ready?"

"We're ready!" Mary said.

CHAPTER 21

FINDING THE CAMP

"Stop!" Eddie shouted, stepping off the wing and backing away from the airplane.

"Wait a minute. Hold everything," Eddie shouted.

"What do you need?" Mary asked.

"You two jump down here for a second, both of you."

"Huh?" Randy asked.

"Come on!"

"What did we do wrong?" Randy asked.

"Oh, it's not you, it's me!" Eddie said. "Get out. We need a plan."

"I thought we were…?" Mary started.

"I've got to give you guys a heads-up," Eddie said.

Randy and Mary crawled out of the front cockpit and jumped to the ground. Mary lifted the goggles from her eyes and strapped them on top of her head. Randy was in his helmet, holding the wire to the earphones.

"Here's the deal," Eddie said. "I'm used to my copilots and guys I fly with having already been trained. I either need to train you two quick or go alone."

"Don't go alone, Eddie," Randy whimpered.

"We'll get nowhere fast and waste time if I don't give you some training," Eddie said.

"We're smart, Eddie," Mary said.

"I know you are, Mary," Eddie said.

"Train us," Mary said.

"Ready?" Eddie asked.

Randy stood at full attention and saluted.

"I'm ready, sir."

"I'm ready," Mary said.

"All right. When we get up there it'll be dark, and we won't be able to hear each other well. If there's no radio systems between us, flyers have to use hand signals. Let me show you. Put your hands together and point them up like this."

Eddie held both hands together high above his head, pointing them straight up.

"This is called twelve o'clock. Just like hands on a clock— twelve o'clock high—up here. It means to look up or fly straight forward. Twelve o'clock low—or down here—is when you point in the opposite direction. It means to descend or look down. Can you do that?"

Both made the twelve o'clock low signal.

"You're doing it right. Now this is what three o'clock looks like, and here's nine o'clock…"

Carefully and patiently Eddie demonstrated to Randy and Mary how to signal him from the front cockpit to indicate which direction he should fly the plane or where to look.

"Won't we do things backwards if we're looking ahead and you're behind us?" Randy asked.

"Good thinking, but you won't be doing it, Randy. Mary will be in front of you directing me where I fly. You're going to be behind her on the radio talking with Sheriff Hood, telling him whatever she tells you to tell him. I want you to know what signals she's giving, too."

Randy beamed.

"Okay, you both have it down," Eddie said.

"Just like hands on a clock," Randy said.

"Mary, have you ever heard about coordinates?"

"Coordinates?"

"Yes."

"If it's not about skirts and blouses, I don't think so," Mary said.

"Okay, I know it's dark, but take a look over there."

Eddie pointed to the road.

"See the coffee percolator setting on the side of the road?"

"Yes."

"Now take a look at the pine tree up on the hill about thirty feet behind us."

"I can see it."

"Now draw an imaginary line from the percolator to the pine tree. Let me know when you can imagine it."

"I got it."

"So, using that line, where is the plane?"

"The line from the pine tree to the percolator goes right through the airplane."

"That's right, so that would be our east-west coordinate for where the plane is."

"I get it," Mary said. "So, now we must find the north and south coordinates for the same plane, so we can pinpoint the X on a map exactly where it is sitting. Am I right?"

"You've got it exactly right, Mary."

"Now what?" Randy asked.

"We'll get her in the air. I'll fly low, maybe fifteen hundred, two thousand feet."

"This is going to be so good," Randy said.

"You two know the area—this part of the Crown?"

"I'm not so sure I do," Mary said.

"I do. I'll help her," Randy said.

"Okay, Randy, you help her. There are a lot of woods around here. Mary, you're going to steer the plane."

"Huh? No way! I don't know how to use that stick," Mary said.

"Not the joystick, Mary. Put all the seat cushions on the floor in the front cockpit and kneel on them so you're up taller than the front windscreen. You give me the clock signals. You'll be telling me where to fly—which way to turn. I'll fly the plane. You take me any which way you want me to go until we find a campfire with a wagon."

"I got it. I can do that."

"Okay, face forward and show me a signal to bank right," Eddie said.

Mary gave the signal for three o'clock.

"Now, a bank left."

Mary showed the signal for nine o'clock.

"After you tell me to bank, Mary, make sure to grab and hold onto the windscreen so you don't fall out."

Over and over they practiced the arm signals.

"Remember, we won't be able to hear each other up there. Once we find it—their campfire—give me the twelve o'clock high or wave signal or something. Then we'll circle to confirm it."

"What then?" Mary asked.

"If we confirm it's the camp, we'll bank right and go find coordinates to it, east and west, north and south," Eddie said.

"Oh, I get it," Mary said.

"When we find the coordinates, you shout them to Randy, and Randy you radio them to Sheriff Hood."

"I can do that," Randy said. "This is so good."

"The sheriff will plot them on a map and know exactly where the camp is."

"Randy, you know this area better than I do," Mary said. "At first I'm thinking we can start in big circles and then close in until we see the campfire. What do you think?"

"I rode horses with Tall Jerry in a lot of these woods. I think we should start by heading down Pompey Hollow Road," Randy said.

"Why so far?" Mary asked.

"I'm guessing the camp will be in the woods east of that somewhere," Randy said.

"Why?" Mary asked.

"I don't think they'd take the wagon past Cherry Valley."

"Not around here?" Mary asked.

"No way, look around you Mary."

"For what?"

"The Delphi Falls hills here are too steep around the falls. The horses couldn't get the wagon up these hills and cliffs into the woods."

"Makes sense," Mary said.

"You two figure it out. We can cover a lot of ground. You'll just have to show me where you want me to fly, Mary," Eddie said.

"And after we find them, we find the coordinates," Mary said.

"Exactly," Eddie said. "You ready to take her up, Randy?"

"I'm ready sir," Randy snapped a salute.

"Me too," Mary said.

"Where do I sit again?" Randy asked.

"Sit on the seat in the front cockpit, cross-legged so Mary has room in front of you. Gather all the seat cushions and give them to Mary to kneel on the floor. We need her to be able to see over the windscreen."

Eddie wet his finger with his mouth and held it in the air to see which direction the wind was blowing. Planes took off better flying into the wind.

"It looks like we'll be taking off from the other end of this field."

"Is that good?" Randy asked.

"The ride down there will give us a feel of it—how smooth or bumpy it is. Blow the lantern out and bring the lantern with us, Randy, we'll leave her lit down there."

"Why?" Randy asked.

"We'll be flying blind in the dark. We'll need the light from the lantern to help us when we come back and need to land. It'll help us find where the end of the runway is."

Randy blew out the lantern.

"Climb in, get settled, Randy. Mary, you get your cushions set. Lean forward into the front windshield. Hang on to it when we bank. The goggles will let you see in the wind without squinting."

"How come you fly it from the rear cockpit, Eddie?" Randy asked.

"A biplane is a tail-dragger. It sets on the ground, nose high. The pilot sits in the back for a reason. This plane is flown by the seat of the pants. Back there I can feel the slightest change in the plane in flight. Best view of the wings and horizon, too. Helps keep it level."

While the wheels were chocked, Eddie reached up and turned the propeller slowly through all cylinders to prime each with fresh fuel. He would turn it and pause. Turn it again and pause. He stepped up on the wing, reached in and turned the magnetos to the right and left and then climbed down again.

"You sure we can take off in this hayfield?" Randy asked.

"Big wheels. She's at ease in a field if there're no woodchuck holes. No worries."

Randy got comfortable in the front cockpit. Mary adjusted her goggles and looked down the field under the full moon.

"Fasten your helmet and earphones," Eddie shouted.

Randy obliged and strapped the helmet to his chin, earphones on.

This time Eddie grabbed the prop with force, flat-handed, giving her a hard, downward pull. The second time he tried she fired up, coughed and spit smoke. The blades revved. He pulled the chocks from in front of the tires and climbed up into the back cockpit, turning the magnetos to the right.

"Hand me the cord attached to the microphone on your helmet," Eddie shouted.

"What for?" Randy barked.

"You're going to be calling and telling Sheriff Hood the coordinates when Mary finds them. When I plug this into the RCA, you won't need your hands to run the microphone."

"This is so good!" Randy shivered with a grin.

Mary got secure kneeling on the cushions, her head above the windscreen nearly touching the bottom of the upper wing.

Eddie plugged the jack from Randy's earphones and microphone into the two-way.

"Yikes," Randy shouted. "That popped in my ears."

"Well, that means you're live now, buddy. Better watch your language. You got ears all over the county listening in. Well crew, what's say we go find us a campfire?"

"Roger Wilko," Randy barked.

Mary gave a thumb-up.

Eddie eased the throttle forward. The propeller sliced through the air with a roar, the big tires rocking the plane gently forward. Mary's hair was flying back with the prop wind.

"When we get to the end of the field, you jump out, Randy, and light the lantern. Leave it about twenty feet from the end of the field. We'll use that as a landing spot when we come back," Eddie shouted.

Randy gave a thumb-up.

The plane rolled down the length of the field. The full moon lighted some of the way not darkened by tree shade. When it reached the end, Eddie touched the stick and the plane turned near full circle, now facing back the other way, awaiting takeoff. Randy started to climb out of his cockpit with the unlit lantern.

"Stay put, Randy."

"What!?"

"Second thoughts! I don't want you walking into the prop. It's easy to do if you don't know the plane. Too dangerous. You both sit still. I'll put the lantern out there."

Eddie climbed out and stepped down onto the field. The plane was rolling slowly. He quickly pulled shorn hay stalks from the ground down to dirt so the lantern could be stable and wouldn't get blown over by wind, causing a fire. He lit the lantern and set it firmly on the space he cleared and crawled back on the wing and into his cockpit. He circled back around to just over the lantern.

"Here we go!" he yelled. "We're flying on your signals from here on out, Mary."

FULL POWER! Pointed straight down the hay lot runway, Eddie eased forward on the stick. Randy was pushed back in his seat with the pressure. Mary was hugging the windscreen. The tail lifted off the ground, levelling the plane on two wheels, gaining speed. Eddie eased back on the stick, lowering the wing flaps, thirty miles per hour, forty miles per hour, fifty, sixty, and off they lifted. The plane floated up, weightless.

Randy's heart bounced like a somersault.

Mary clung to the windshield and grinned. It was almost like she could reach out and touch the treetops. Up, up, over the tip of the trees next to the bridge, over the creek. She looked over at the lower Delphi Falls to the left, then the upper falls as the plane climbed higher over Farmer Parker's side pasture hill. Above the trees in the moonlight they saw the reflections of white and black Holstein cows around the pasture. Mary could see Buddy's gravestone. As the plane rose into the sky, the lights below as far as the hamlet and Gooseville corners sparkled like stars. The full moon's reflection settled on the wing of the plane almost within reach.

Randy gripped the side of the cockpit with his elbow, taking it in as if he was on a magic carpet. He leaned his head down and watched sights he had only dreamed about. The engine whined and roared.

Still climbing, Eddie leaned forward, reached up and tapped Randy on the shoulder.

"Call the sheriff and let him know we're up and looking. Tell him we'll report in when we find something."

"How do I do that?" Randy shouted.

"It's on your helmet," Eddie shouted.

"This mic?" Randy asked.

"That's it. Yes! Find the button on it."

"I found it!"

"Just touch that button when you want to talk. Release it to listen. You'll hear through your earphones."

"This is Randy calling," Randy shouted into the mic. "This is Randy calling Sheriff Todd Hood, come in, Sheriff Hood."

With a scratch and hiss…

"Come in, Randy. Read you loud and clear. This is Sheriff Todd Hood, come back."

Randy about had a heart attack. But it wasn't long before he got the hang of it.

The moon shined off the propeller blades like icicles cutting through the sky.

The whine of the engine was steady, pistons beating like a snare drum leading a parade.

Mary looked through the spinning prop with a gleam in her eyes and thought of Amelia Earhart flying alone across the Atlantic in 1928.

"Sheriff Hood, we're airborne," Randy shouted. "I'll give you coordinates to where the campfire is when we find it. This is Randy, over."

"Randy, this is Sheriff Hood, we'll wait. Be careful, over."

Mary looked for a landmark she would recognize.

There it was—the Pompey Hollow Road.

She decided to take Randy's advice. The area east of the road was the most wooded. If that didn't work, she would have the plane circle around and look over the Delphi Falls at Big Mike's place.

Mary signaled ten o'clock, grabbed the windscreen and Eddie obliged, banking the plane a slight left.

184

"Hang on!" Eddie shouted.

The plane would first tilt and then angle weightless in the sky. Once over the road, Mary signaled twelve o'clock level. The plane rolled back and over the middle of the Pompey Hollow Road they flew, two thousand feet up. Just past spinster Nettie's house Mary thought she saw a glow off to the right. She turned her head around and got Eddie's attention by pointing down to the glow of a fire. Eddie nodded. He could see it.

"Hang on!" Eddie shouted.

He banked the plane into a slight dive to take a closer look. It was a campfire.

Ole Charlie here couldn't have been prouder.

Eddie circled twice to be certain it was Marty's camp. There it surely was, a campfire, a wagon and two horses looking a bit nervous about the sounds overhead. Eddie banked back out and waited for Mary's next signal to start finding coordinates.

"This is Randy calling Sheriff Hood. Randy calling Sheriff Hood. Come in, please."

"Sheriff Todd Hood, here. Come back, Randy."

"We've found the camp, Sheriff, come back."

"Good job folks, come back."

"Spread a map and I'll send coordinates for you to rule in, come back."

"Roger and over."

There were scratching noises in Randy's ears.

Mary signaled three o'clock and the biplane banked to the right. Getting comfortable with the motion she leaned with the plane like it was a flying bicycle. She then pointed twelve o'clock forward and it levelled off. As soon as she could make out a farm and silo below, she turned her head and shouted.

"Randy, whose farm is that?"

"Where?" Randy shouted.

"That one down there."

"Barber's," he shouted.

Mary signaled that their barn would be the first coordinate. She then signaled to Eddie to fly straight from the farm back up over the campfire and then to keep going up the tall hill.

"Come in, Sheriff Hood. Come in Sheriff Hood."

"This is Sheriff Hood, come in, Randy."

"First coordinate is Barber's farm. Come back."

"Roger that. Barber's farm, over."

The engine roared as they flew up over the heavily wooded hill, passed over the campfire, and then saw ahead of them the lights of Cazenovia, sparkling under a full moon. Mary signaled back to Eddie to turn around.

"Hang on!" Eddie shouted.

The plane banked into a turn.

"Brae Loch Inn," Mary shouted back to Randy.

He gave her a thumbs-up, hearing her.

"Sheriff Hood, this is Randy, come back."

"Come in, Randy. Sheriff Hood here."

"Barber's farm up to Brae Loch Inn is the first coordinate, Sheriff, come back."

"Roger that, Randy. Barbers' farm to Brae Loch Inn. Over."

As the plane banked right, Mary signaled and pointed the plane over to and around the second Delphi Falls. The waterfalls glistened under the moon. Looking down at the falls, Mary got her bearings and signaled another bank toward the campfire, looking straight down for another landmark. Sighting one, she turned her head toward Randy and pointed down.

Randy nodded and pushed the button on his mic.

"This is Randy calling Sheriff Hood. Come in, Sheriff Hood."

"Sheriff Hood here, Randy. Come back."

"Burlingame Road at the Cobb Hill Road connection, Sheriff. Do you read?"

"Corner of Burlingame Road and Cobb Hill Road. Have it, Randy. I read you loud and clear."

Mary gave a thumbs-up and pointed the plane straight toward and over the campfire glow again. Soon after she reached a final coordinate—one she recognized. She pointed down at it, getting Randy's attention.

"Randy calling Sheriff Hood. Come in, Sheriff."

"This is Sheriff Hood, read you loud and clear, Randy. Come back."

"The crossing of Oran Delphi and Cherry Valley. Do you read me, Sheriff Hood? The crossing of Oran Delphi and Cherry Valley!"

"Read you loud and clear. Burlingame Road and Cobb Hill Road over to Oran Delphi and Cherry Valley. We know exactly where the camp is now. Good job all of you. Come back."

"This is Randy, Mary, and Flying Eddie signing off."

"Fly safe. This is Sheriff Todd Hood signing off. Over and out."

Mary signalled Eddie to bank a left in a circle and turn up the Oran Delphi heading for the hamlet, and then the hayfield back home at the Delphi Falls.

"Hang on!" Eddie shouted. "We're going home."

Mary had a contented smile on her face looking up at the bright stars, the full moon, her hair flowing behind her.

Randy rubbed his hands together briskly to warm them in the cold night air. He was enjoying this adventure of a lifetime.

Eddie was shivering in the cold, but warmed by the thought of getting his money back and flying to Binghamton and his family. He steadied the stick between his knees, looking up at the moon and feeling the wind on his face. Mary turned around, caught his eye and gave him a thumb-up.

He looked down at a bag next to his seat, looked up at Mary, and with two hands cupped over his mouth.

"Mary, is there a lake near here?"

"A lake?" she shouted back.

"A lake, yes," Eddie shouted.

"Water?"

"Yes," Eddie nodded.

Mary gave the twelve o'clock sign to fly straight and follow Oran Delphi Road over the hamlet to the water. A mile or so past Gooseville Corners would be DeRuyter Lake, the reservoir popular in the summer for fishing and swimming.

As the moon glistened on the glassy still water of the lake, Eddie banked the plane left and circled the lake, bringing the plane down to a thousand feet.

"What are you doing?" Mary shouted.

Randy looked around, his eyes as big as quarters wondering what was going on as well.

"Eddie! What are you doing?" Mary shouted again.

"This!" Eddie shouted.

He opened the paper sack and held up an unopened bottle of whiskey he had next to his seat. As the plane glided over the middle of the lake, he threw the bottle over.

"Won't need that anymore," he shouted as the bottle hurled down and splashed into the middle of the lake.

Mary grinned and gave him another thumb-up.

"Proud of you, Eddie!" she shouted.

"Turn around, Mary, and find us that lantern and the end of that field," Eddie shouted. "So we can land this thing. I need a hot cup of coffee."

With a smile on her face, Mary turned to the front, pointed to one o'clock and hung onto the windscreen for a bank right.

CHAPTER 22

THE JIG IS UP

Eddie was landing safely back by the Delphi Falls about the time the pickpocket was in the telephone closet at the Lincklaen House doing business with, unbeknown to him, his foil, Myrtie.

As to Duba, who was still fast asleep outside, ain't much to say other than young'uns can be angels when they're sleeping.

Duba was just that, conked out the way he was. He'd been in a deep sleep since sunset. His jowl was pressed up against the side window of his pickup, his lower lip wrigglin' with each breath he took, a fog clouding the window over his nostrils.

Pickpocket stepped from the hotel and looked about. He noticed the TAXI sign in the back of the truck and rapped his knuckles on the window. Duba startled and about sprained his neck opening his eyes and waking up.

"Are you for hire?" the pickpocket asked.

He spoke in a loud enough tone to be heard through the window.

Duba rose to the occasion as best he could, sitting up.

"Huh?"

"I noticed the taxi sign in the back of your truck, mate."

"Oh." Duba said.

"Are you for hire at this hour?"

"For hire?" Duba mumbled, wiping drool from his chin.

"I need a lift," the pickpocket said.

"Sure—for hire—that's right. For hire. Jump in," Duba snorted, trying to shake his sleep off.

The pickpocket stepped around in front of the truck carrying a large satchel as Duba pulled the headlights on. A red carnation, a beret and all just as Duba remembered him on the Midway, the scoundrel made it around to the passenger side door when Duba realized he still had Sheriff Hood's copy of the map on his lap. A dead giveaway, if ever the pickpocket saw it. He bolted, crumpled it up and stuck it down the front of his pants as the door opened.

"Put the bag in the back, if you want. It won't go anywhere."

"I'd rather keep it with me, if is all the same to you, Gov."

"No matter to me."

Duba realized it was probably filled with money.

"Thank you."

Pickpocket climbed in and set the satchel on the floor between his legs. Duba started the truck and put it in gear, ready to back into the Lincklaen House drive, to turn around.

"It won't take long, fella," Duba said. "You'll be there in no time at all."

"Be there? Be where?"

Duba suddenly realized he wasn't supposed to know where they were going. He caught himself with a silent gulp.

"My good man, won't you need to know where I might be going first?"

"Well ah, yes, that's what I meant to say, that is, when you tell me where you need to go, you see, and after that, I'll get you there. Fast, ya see. I mean…"

Duba shook his head, stretched his eyelids wide, rolling his eyeballs in circles while slapping on his cheeks to wake up.

"I have a map of instructions," the pickpocket said. "I can't quite make it out. If you know the area you might be able to read it."

Duba stepped on the brake in the middle of the driveway and took the pickpocket's map from the envelope and unfolded it. He did the best he could to look at it as if he was studying it. He held it

191

up close to his eyes, examining the paper, its authenticity. Lad was overacting now that he almost blew his cover before.

"See that X there?"

"The X?"

"Right here on the map. See it?"

"I do, actually. Yes, I see it."

"I know where that spot is," Duba said.

"I say, good go!" the pickpocket said.

"It's a popular campsite for people traveling through," Duba said.

"I see," the pickpocket said.

"Apple orchards all about it."

The pickup finished backing into the Lincklaen House driveway to turn around and head to Albany Street.

This was when Duba felt he needed more mystery and began his small talk.

"In town on business, are you?"

The pickpocket didn't answer.

Duba was a bundle of nerves, knowing he had slept through everything and failed to get the map to the sheriff.

"What time is it, anyway?" Duba asked.

The pickpocket pulled a pocket watch from his vest pocket and held it up to the dashboard to read.

"It's eight o'clock," the pickpocket said.

"Right on time," Duba mumbled.

"Pardon me? What did you mean 'right on time?' Were you expecting me, mate?"

"Huh?" Duba grunted. "Right—what did you say? On time?"

"No, you said it."

"No. I said right…on Albany Street…then it's left down at the end. Right was for Albany Street…"

"I beg your pardon, Gov. It's been a long day and I've been hearing things lately."

"In town on business, are you?" Duba asked, while beads of perspiration gathered on his forehead.

"I'm with a traveling troupe of theater players. I play Sherlock Holmes in *The Final Adventure*. It's a stage play. Are you an Arthur Conan Doyle or Sherlock Holmes fan? I have tickets if you are?"

"Oh, I read a Sherlock Holmes book…about the dogs…"

"*The Hound of the Baskervilles*. It's a marvellous intrigue," the pickpocket said.

"I liked it," Duba said. "Lots of dogs and stuff."

"Curious take on it," the pickpocket said.

"I liked him, Sherlock Holmes and his doctor friend."

"Doctor Watson."

"That's him."

"Indeed, yes."

Still waking up, fretting about Sheriff Hood without a map, Duba was in a daze but still somehow star-struck.

"So, you're the Sherlock Holmes?"

"At your service, at least on stage, I am," Sherlock Holmes snapped.

The pickup turned onto Cherry Valley and started the steep climb before going down to the Pompey Hollow Road turnoff.

"Lots of fog in England, is there?" Duba asked.

"We're surrounded by water," Sherlock Holmes said.

"Like Long Island, I guess," Duba said.

Sherlock Holmes looked over at Duba, puzzled, trying to make the connection between Long Island and England.

"That's where our potatoes come from mostly," Duba said.

"I see," Sherlock Holmes said.

Sherlock did a double take.

"Oh, I get it now. Your Long Island. It's an island, like Great Britain. I get your point."

Duba was slowing down to turn on Pompey Hollow Road.

Completely at a loss for what to do, and thinking Sheriff Hood was in the dark about where the camp was, Duba tried to invent solutions on his own.

"Do you want me to wait?"

"Yes, please," Sherlock Holmes said. "It shouldn't be long."

"I'll wait, then."

"Would you mind terribly?"

"I'll wait."

Duba slowed down before spinster Nettie's house and cautiously turned in on the dirt path that would lead to Marty's camp. He was fifty yards in when they could hear the low whinny of the horses. Another fifty yards and they could see the glow of a campfire lighting up the canvas-covered wagon.

Ole Charlie here rose up and rested on a maple tree branch above the wagon and behind the campfire to watch.

The horses were tied up to the right of the wagon and Marty and Jerry were sitting by the campfire staring into it, cool as cucumbers, pretending to take no notice of Duba's pickup driving in. The truck pulled to a stop. The headlights turned off. Duba sat in the truck, sweating the worst while Sherlock Holmes stepped out carrying his satchel. He walked toward the campfire.

"Lovely night," Sherlock Holmes said.

"Good moon," Marty mumbled, while holding his coffee tin with both hands for warmth.

Marty sat sipping coffee, looking at the fire. Tall Jerry was pretending he liked it.

"I'm here to do business," Sherlock Holmes said.

"Need some water, do you?" Marty asked.

"No water, I'm here..."

"If it's not water you want, what are you doing here?"

"I beg your pardon?"

"We don't have enough food cooked to share," Marty snorted.

"We pretty much ate it all," Tall Jerry said.

"Thank you, no. I ate with the troupe earlier."

"Troop?" You a soldier, are ya?" Marty asked.

"Oh my, no, it's an acting troupe. Easy enough mistake. I'm Sherlock Holmes, don't ya' see, in New Woodstock tomorrow."

"Sherlock Holmes, eh," Marty said. "So why are you here in my camp, Sherlock?"

"I don't quite understand," Sherlock said. "I brought my money to exchange for your counterfeit, just as we said."

"Don't know what you're talking about. I find water for people. A séance now and then if need be."

Sitting there listening to this bantering, Tall Jerry was getting edgy. He bit on his lip.

"Oh, right," Sherlock said. "I get it now—the séance thing. The lady on the telly gave me the clue. I'm supposed to say I'm here for the séance."

"Remembering that could have saved a lot of time," Marty said. "How much did you bring?"

Sherlock knelt and opened his leather bag and tipped it so Marty and Tall Jerry could look inside. It had a pile of wallets and loose cash.

Relieved that he had finally connected, Sherlock stood, patted the palm of his hand on his chest, took a deep breath and sighed.

"Oh my, I brought enough, I'm sure."

"We'll see," Marty said.

"I believe we were talking one thousand American for five thousand of yours."

"None of my business, but where's a guy like you get all those wallets and all that money? Not that I care."

"Lots of folk daydreaming while walking about the fair's Midway distractions, not paying attention to business. Carnivals are ripe, too. I pay attention to my business a little better," Sherlock smirked.

"And your business is?" Marty asked.

"Oh, I'm an actor by trade, but it's thin pickings, acting is, mate. Lifting a pocket or two pays the lights, shall we say?"

"You mean stealing," Marty said.

"I like to call it removing blokes from the temptations of sin. You know those horrific sideshows—naked trollops and such. The buggers may go home broke, but they can go home to the Mrs. with clear consciences."

"Pretty smart. Most people, even thieves, have to work to earn their money to buy my product. You got no cost or sweat in your money at all, stealing it to begin with."

"So, we can do business, mate?"

"Your counterfeit money is bundled and in the back of the wagon."

"Loose in the back?"

"It's a package wrapped with twine in the big trunk."

"Is there a key?"

"The lock's open."

"I see."

"Count it carefully. Make sure it's all there, and you're happy."

"Oh, I shall."

"I don't make refunds."

"Do I pay now?"

"Pay me after you count it."

"Should I leave my satchel with you?"

"No, take it with you. I don't want to take chances of anyone seeing all those wallets. 'Sides, you ain't going to run off anywhere until I get my money," Marty said. "We know the woods better."

Sherlock looked at Marty, then he nodded his head over at Duba, sitting behind the wheel of the truck.

"You mean he's…?" Sherlock asked.

"He works for me," Marty said. "Go count your money, make sure it's five thousand, then come pay me the thousand you owe me."

Sherlock Holmes smiled at the organization Marty had. It gave him confidence Marty was on the level, and that his counterfeit bills would be high quality. He saluted, tipping his brow, took two steps back and turned, looking at the horses munching the broken hay bales. He found his way around to the back side of the wagon and pushed the canvas tarp curtain aside.

A flashlight beamed in his face, startling him.

"Put your hands up, Mr. Sherlock Holmes!" Sheriff Hood barked from inside the wagon. "Put both hands in the air, now. You're under arrest!"

He was pointing his pistol at Sherlock Holmes.

Sheriff Hood crawled to the back end of the wagon, stepped down and whistled.

Out from behind trees and other hiding places in the woods came Holbrook, Randy, Dick, Conway, and Dwyer. Alice was sitting in Conway's car.

Sheriff Hood handcuffed Sherlock and walked him around to the campfire.

"It's not a fair cop, Gov," Sherlock barked.

"Think not?" Sheriff Hood asked.

"You can't arrest me for buying counterfeit. No money exchanged hands. I'll get a solicitor."

"That's a good point," the sheriff said.

"So uncuff me, Gov, and I'm gone."

"I'm not arresting you for counterfeiting. I'm arresting you for theft. You're a pickpocket. We can prove that. You just admitted to it. I'm a witness. I heard the whole thing from the wagon. That's the same as a confession, and that's grand larceny."

"None of those wallets will have more than a few dollars."

"What's your point?"

"That's not grand larceny then, Gov. You'll never get me on grand larceny for a couple of quid," Sherlock snarled.

"Maybe only a few dollars in each of those wallets, but honest, hard-earned dollars, and they'll all have names in them—the owner's names. Why some of those wallets are heirlooms, I have a feeling. All they have to do is press charges."

Sheriff Hood opened the pickpocket's satchel. He lifted out a manila envelope and tore it open.

"Hmmm. Looks like six hundred and forty dollars in this envelope alone. Unless you have a good reason for these six hundred and forty dollars, this makes it grand larceny."

"That's my money, Gov. Ahhh…it's the ticket money for the Sherlock Holmes Players performance tomorrow. Every quid in that envelope was my money."

Sheriff reached deeper into the same manila envelope and lifted out a smaller envelope that was sealed.

"Well look what we have here. These are torn coupon ticket receipts for airplane rides," Sheriff Hood said. "Looks like a few dozen of them. Doesn't say anything about any Sherlock Holmes' play on them. I'm supposing you can show me where you park your airplane for plane rides, can you?"

Sherlock dropped his head in defeat.

It was a few minutes when Barber drove the sheriff's car into the open. Other cars came out of the woods. Sheriff Hood walked the pickpocket to his car.

"After you, Sherlock…and watch your head," he said while locking the crook in the back seat.

He was about to take the scoundrel to a lockup.

As he was putting the leather bag of evidence into his trunk he paused. He walked over to Marty.

"Marty, I believe this envelope—the money and coupons— belongs to Eddie. No need to do paperwork. The proof's strong it's all his. See to it he gets it, will you?"

"Sure will, Sheriff," Marty said. "I'll be more than happy to."

"And thank you guys and gals for everything. You all were good at pulling this off."

"It was close, but we pulled it off," Dick said.

"Oh, and thank Eddie, Randy, and Mary for getting the coordinates to me at the last minute like they did."

"What do you mean, coordinates?" Dick asked.

"We'd have been lost without them."

"What do you mean?" Dick asked.

Didn't you get the map Mr. Ossant left?" Tall Jerry asked. "I saw the envelope in his hand when they left here?"

"It wasn't there," Sheriff Hood said.

Duba walked up carrying his handmade TAXI sign.

"I wonder what happened to the sheriff's map?" Dick asked.

Duba swallowed a gulp and threw the taxi sign into the campfire, setting it ablaze.

Lifting the harnesses, Marty looked at Duba as Dick stepped in to help.

"Beats me," Duba said, "I'll have to ask around—up at the hotel." He turned his back, pulled the crumpled envelope and map from the front of his pants and dropped them on the fire, blocking their view until they were ablaze. The lad wasn't one to keep secrets from Dick, but now was not the time to share.

Marty hitched up the horses. He and Tall Jerry doused the campfire with coffee, a jug of water and some dirt, and climbed on the wagon. Following Conway's taillights, they drove the team out of the woods, turned left onto Pompey Hollow Road and headed back toward Farmer Parker's farm.

"Sheriff Hood," Dick said. "The pickpocket has three hundred dollars of Big Mike's and Mike Shea's money. The doc's, too. Can we get it now?"

"They'll get it back. I have some paperwork to fill out, but they'll get it all back. Did you happen to mark the bills like you did for the store burglars?"

"We were afraid to," Dick said. If we got him thinking it was counterfeit, he might have inspected the bills close up and maybe seen a mark."

"That was smart," Sheriff Hood said.

In single file the cars made their way through the winding dirt road around trees and out of the woods down to Pompey Hollow Road, following the horses and wagon up ahead. No one was in any hurry. It was a slow parade of cars, with windows open—laughing, cheering and singing. There were lots of smiles glowing in the moonlight, celebrating another victory for the Pompey Hollow Book Club.

CHAPTER 23

SIGN FROM ABOVE

This was about when the *moonstruck* happened—first time ever for ole Charlie here. I decided to stay at Marty's and Tall Jerry's campsite and sit a spell on this here maple tree branch. The fire was out, but I had the full moon to reflect on, and I wanted time to reflect. Angels do that sort of thing—count our blessin's, as be said.

Sheriff Hood was the last to drive out of the camp. He turned right on Pompey Hollow Road. He was on his way to locking up the young lad overnight in Cazenovia and moving him to the county jail the next day to wait for a judge.

It was just as the sheriff was at the end of Pompey Hollow Road making his turn onto Cherry Valley that I first saw it. The full moon. It flickered twice.

Can you imagine?

Not just a blink of the eye, mind you, but the moon—turnin' on and off like it was a kitchen light bulb. It sure enough flickered full out, twice. I know you'll find it hard to believe, but just so you won't be in the dark, you should know the only body what could see a flickering of the moon like that are guardian angels. But to be clear, not just any guardian angel can see the flickering, neither.

Moon flickering is heaven's calling an Angel Congress, sure enough, but only for angels who could see it. That'd be me tonight, no telling who else, but I'm guessing since this Sherlock Holmes actor is involved, I'm guessing Sir Arthur Conan Doyle can see the moon flickering as well. It was signalling for an Angel Congress on top of Big Mike's barn garage roof at Delphi Falls.

I somehow almost magically appeared on top of Big Mike's barn garage that quick. Floating up the front side of the roof, I could see across the way, the horses, wagon, the cars pulling into Farmer Parkers.

On the other side of the roof it was darker, with the moon to our backs. The white rock high on the cliff across the creek seemed to reflect a glow.

He was sitting there all prim and proper, studying his pocket watch glass off a beam of the moon. Waiting for me was none other than Sir Arthur Conan Doyle. My mentor on subjects once foreign to me, and now a friend.

As a courtesy I waited for him to speak first.

He caught my eye. Then he looked at the white rock up on the cliff across the creek, aglow under the moon.

"The lad's name is Dudley Smythe," Sir Doyle said. "He was born on Bond Street in London, not all that far from me; a decent, respectable, proper family."

"Do tell."

"Seems young Dudley had just turned fifteen, when he, his sister, mother, and father all took cover in a 1942 London blackout. The sirens were wailing. They hurried down to the basement under their four-story London flat when a German U2 bomb dropped from the sky and destroyed his family home, shattering two adjacent homes and a school just across the park. The house foundation dislodged, and a falling wooden beam timber killed his parents instantly while he watched. His sister lost her left arm from a tetanus infection she got cutting herself on a metal piece of shrapnel she fell onto in the basement."

Ole Charlie here was stunned.

Sir Doyle continued.

"Times were not easy in London all throughout the war. Orphans now, Dudley and his sister were separated and shuffled about from home to home. Food was scarce. The boy loved to read, but he was belligerent, incorrigible, kept running away whenever he could. He became a roustabout, picking up odd jobs, quitting school, stealing books, sleeping in alleys and parks. He's never come to grips with losing his parents the way he did. He won't forgive anyone for his sister losing her arm, as he sarcastically puts it, 'losing her wedding ring finger to a trash barrel.'"

"Above wants you to be his guardian angel now, don't they, Sir Doyle? I have that feeling."

"I will be the second you take me to him, Charlie. He appeared in your kingdom first—how do you put it, the Crown? The Almighty has given you the power to transition him to me."

Now it's not like ole Charlie here to get all persnickety like I was about to, but I felt I had to hold my ground.

"I'm humbled. I'll gladly do it, Sir Doyle, but I have a condition, if I might."

"Condition, Charlie? Are you in any position to…? What might your condition be, my friend?"

"That you be the guardian angel for his sister, too, is all. I don't know where she is nor what her state is, but the poor girl needs you as well, I'm thinking."

Sir Doyle smiled.

He looked up at the glowing white rock on the cliff across the creek. That was a sign. Angels on high approved Sir Doyle being the sister's guardian angel.

Sir Doyle tightened his lips and looked down pensively.

"It was a magician doing card tricks on the streets of London that found him."

"Imagine that."

"Young Dudley would stand beside his sidewalk table, watch his fingers move and his palms curl. He could always tell which card the pea was under."

"The lad showed a daring on the Midway, Sir Doyle."

"The magician took the lad under his wing. Oh, a scoundrel he was! He taught young Dudley how to lift pockets with the best of them. He gave him books to keep him happy, tailor-clothed him to look the part of a gentleman, and gave him a bed, and one meal a day. When the lad was to his liking, he put him on the better streets of London from dawn until sunset to line his own pockets with Dudley's daily take."

"Dawn to dusk."

"Oh, he'd slap the lad soundly, he would, even hold his supper from him if he didn't bring enough booty each day. On the back-street bars and alleys away from the upper-class parts of London he was called 'Dudley the Dipper.'"

"Poor lad. I thought he was an actor."

"He is, and a decent one. He picked it up while he was lifting the pockets of theater-goers. He'd read Sherlock Holmes novels over and over to see if he could learn how to get around the law—be above it. Reading so many stories he literally became Sherlock Holmes gone awry."

"Can you save him, Sir Doyle?"

"Only he can save himself, Charlie. He looks to the Sherlock Holmes players as his family, now. Maybe they can help. I can watch over him and must," Sir Doyle said.

"Having a guardian angel gives the soul ballast, conscience, Sir Doyle."

"We'll see. Time will tell."

"I'll help you any way I can, Sir Doyle. Bless you for helping me through the week."

"I may have questions for you about systems and procedures here in America, Charlie."

"If I know, I'll give you answers."

"Can I ask you to take me to where our young Dudley might be, transition him to me and stay through the ordeal until I am acclimated?"

"Of course, my friend. Let's go."

With that, ole Charlie here seemed to know what to do, don't ask me how. I raised my arm and without having to think about it, both Sir Arthur Conan Doyle and I appeared in the center office of the Cazenovia courthouse and jail. Sheriff Hood was sitting on one side of the wooden table while the pickpocket Dudley Smythe was sitting on the other side, with a cigarette in his mouth.

We sat on top of the filing cabinets to observe.

Sheriff Hood was making a point.

"This will go a lot easier on you if you cooperate. What's your name?"

"Yer the copper, Gov - find it yer own self."

"You don't want to help?"

"Why should I make it cushy for you?"

"Because I have twenty-five wallets and four ladies' purses," Sheriff Hood said.

"What's it to me?"

"We're looking at four hundred and thirty dollars here, plus the six hundred and forty you stole from the airplane ride pilot."

"So?"

"Grand larceny in this state will get you two to twenty-one years in prison."

"I found that bag with all of them in it. I'll swear to it. You can't prove otherwise."

"You've already confessed to picking pockets on the Midway."

"I don't know why you're holding me. You got no case, Gov. Nobody can prove I took anything. I found them, and I was about to turn them in."

"I have a witness, son."

"You've got nobody, copper."

"Remember the lady in the wheelchair?"

Dudley raised his eyes up.

"So what if I do?"

"She's a fourth-grade school teacher, and a good actor."

205

"I don't believe you."

"How many days do you think she was watching you?"

"What do you mean?"

"Watching you pick pockets on the Midway?"

Dudley the pickpocket lit another cigarette.

Angel Sir Doyle nudged the sheriff by stirring up a breeze that shuffled papers on a side desk. The sheriff stood and lifted a paperweight to set on the papers blowing about when he noticed handwriting of earlier notes about the pickpocket. They were Dick and Duba's notes from the library that said he first spoke in a French accent, pretending he was Vichy French. The sheriff read them, turned, tweaked his chin with his thumb and finger, thinking. He lifted a leg and placed his foot on his chair, looking across the table at Sherlock.

"Here's what's going to happen now, Sherlock Holmes," Sheriff Hood said.

Feeling the jig might be up, Dudley raised his eyes, looking up at the sheriff.

"Or would you prefer to be called "Monsieur Holmes?" John asked.

Dudley was jolted. He stiffened his back.

"We know about your cover, pretending you're French."

Sheriff Hood saw the squirm. He tried again.

"Dudley, I'm sure you have a mother and a father somewhere who will worry about you when they find out you're locked up."

"Shut your gab," Dudley said.

"Most likely some sisters and brothers," the sheriff prodded.

"Shut up."

"I'm going to lock you in a cell so you can think about them— your mother, your father, and your sister, and what you're doing to their name."

Dudley's shoulders slumped.

"While you think it over I'm going to the Lincklaen House and ask your actor friends about you. I'm sure they'll tell me what I need to know."

Pickpocket stared down blankly at the table top.

Seeing his angst, the sheriff tried again.

"Want to tell me your father's name so we can contact him?"

"What does your mother like to cook for holidays?

"Do you have a sister? Is she married? Any brothers?"

"Okay, okay, Sheriff, enough."

"I won't be long talking to your actor friends."

"I'll spill, Sheriff. I'll tell you what you need. Just ask me. I'll tell you straight—I promise—anything you want to know. Leave the actors out of this."

"Too late," Sheriff Hood said. "You had your chance."

"Please, Gov—not my friends—I'll talk."

Ole Charlie here looked over at Sir Doyle. He had his cheeks resting in the palms of his hands. His fingers were toying with his sideburns. He looked over at me, nodded his head, and then he looked back at his Dudley Smythe.

"Let's start at the beginning," Sheriff Hood said.

"Ask me anything, Gov."

"Are you Vichy French or British? We have to report noncitizen arrests."

"My name is Smythe, Dudley Smythe. I'm British, Gov. I only pretended I was Vichy French so no one would get wise and connect me to my English acting troupe company."

"Are they in on it, the pickpocketing?"

"They're a good lot, they are. They don't know."

"You pretended to be French, what—to cover your tracks?"

"Yeah, that's right, Gov, but not French. Vichy French. The Vichy were those Hitler-loving bastards."

"So, you thought because Vichy France was like an enemy to England during the war, if people thought you were Vichy French, they wouldn't connect you with the actors?"

"That's right, Gov."

Sheriff Hood sat and rested his forearms on the table. He waited for the pickpocket to make the next move.

Slowly, methodically, nearly as if he were in a trance, Dudley Smythe stared down at the table top and began telling the story of how he could remember hearing the bombs from the Blitz, the ground in all of London shaking under their quake beginning in 1939 and all through the war, until 1945. He told of his family hiding in the basement during a blackout and seeing the beam coming ajar and crushing his mother and father as he watched, helpless. He spoke of having to wait in the hospital hallway and hearing his sister screaming as they took her in to cut off her arm. He told of the homes he was in, the many beatings, running away. He told of the magician and the lifting of pockets and the books he had read, and finally running away from him.

"I lifted the wallets, Gov. Every one of 'em."

Sir Doyle rustled the air, loosening more desktop papers.

Sheriff Hood got up, turned and stepped over to catch them. He paged through each page. One was the billboard poster for the Sherlock Holmes Players' performance in New Woodstock, set for tomorrow.

"Starring Dudley Smythe as Sherlock Holmes and his 'family' of players," it said.

Sheriff Hood set the poster down under the weight and stepped back to the table, thinking.

"And the players had no part in any of your thefts?"

"Not a lick. I swear. They've been a family to me—the lot of them."

Sir Doyle smiled, knowing the sheriff was thinking this through. The clue of the simple word 'family' was helping it come together— to make sense to him.

208

"Okay, in the cell you go," the sheriff said. "I have some thinking to do."

"I told you the truth, Gov. Honest I did."

Sheriff Hood took Dudley by the elbow and led him into a cell, locking the door.

"I'll get you some food. You must be hungry."

"I'm sorry I got cheeky with you, Gov. You're a good bloke."

Sheriff Hood pulled his jacket on and walked out of the courthouse, locking the door behind him. He crossed Albany Street, turned up the sidewalk and into the lobby of the Lincklaen House. At the front desk he slapped on the bell two times.

She had come from the dining room next to the lobby from putting linens on tables preparing for tomorrow.

"May I help you, Sheriff?" the night clerk asked.

"You have some actors here from England—the Sherlock Holmes actors?"

"We do," the clerk said.

"I need to see them all."

"Is there trouble, Sheriff?"

"How about I use the back room—the one behind the dining area fireplace? That should be secluded enough."

"Please, Sheriff, is there any trouble?" the night clerk asked.

"I need to talk with those folks. Can you call them down?"

"Yes, of course. I'll call their rooms. They're all sharing two rooms. If they're not in their room, I'll check the Seven Stone Steps pub below."

Sheriff Hood looked at his wristwatch. It was nearing midnight.

"I'll go wait," Sheriff Hood said. "Thank you."

While Sheriff Hood waited to meet the Sherlock Holmes players at the Lincklaen House, a celebration with laughter and merriment was taking place at Farmer Parker's. They were standing and sitting with paper plates in their hands, recounting the adventure. Eddie's satchel was on display in the middle of the table, as a prize.

"What time are you taking off tomorrow, Eddie?" Marty asked.

"I'm thinking midmorning," Eddie said. "I could use some sun, flying in this cold air."

"Your girls are going to be so happy," Mary said.

"No more so than my seeing them."

"They'll get to see their daddy."

"Eddie," Farmer Parker said, "you're welcome to use the phone and call them tonight or in the morning, to let them know you're coming."

"I thought about it, Farmer Parker. I think I want to surprise them."

"You're nervous," Mary said. "Don't forget what I told you about daddy's little girls. There's no need to be nervous."

"I bet pickpocket is nervous," Holbrook said. "I wonder if they're making him sweat and confess under hot lights."

"You mean Sherlock Holmes," Barber said.

"I wonder what happened to the map I left for him," Marty said. "It was marked 'Messenger.' I remember seeing all three envelopes. The girl had mine and another two. I wonder what happened to Sheriff Hood's."

"Randy and I got to fly around tonight," Mary said. "It was so amazing flying low. It felt like we could reach out and touch the trees."

"Eddie, you're a great pilot. I'll say!" Randy said.

"We saw you buzzing the camp," Marty said.

"Yeah," Tall Jerry said. We weren't sure if the pickpocket was walking in and could see us, so we pretended not to notice you doing it."

Big Mike rapped his knuckles on the window and walked in.

"Hi, folks," Big Mike said. "Not here to spoil the party. Myrtie told us all the news. Well done…Wanted you to know, folks are planning a celebration and going-away party for you tomorrow, Eddie. Eleven o'clock—our place. Sheriff Hood will be there with some words to say. We've called each of your parents; they said you can stay over tonight. Tomorrow being Sunday, all of them were okay with it. Mary, your dad said to tell you he'll deliver your papers."

That pretty much settled it. The club was staying over. Eddie was about to have a party before he took off. Wasn't a soul there not in favor of it, including Eddie.

"Eddie, are you crying?" Mary asked. "Don't cry, be happy. We got your money back, just like we promised. It's going to be a great Christmas."

Eddie tightened his lip, looked up at the ceiling, nodding his head yes at Mary. It was his thank-you.

Jerry interrupted, tapping on his glass with a spoon with a toast.

"Here's to Eddie, a full-fledged member of the Pompey Hollow Book Club!"

"Hear! Hear!" Dick said, raising his glass of milk in a toast. "The club and us SOS boys just kicked butt and took names."

"Quit hogging the bacon," Barber said. "Randy, grab the bacon plate from Bases. Pass it over here, will ya?"

CHAPTER 24

A RIGHT PROPER SEND-OFF

Big Mike brought boxes of warm, glazed donuts from the bakery. All lined up around the dining room table for the taking, and large pots of hot chocolate with ladles and a big urn of coffee he borrowed from Leonard's Coffee Shop in Homer. Sugar piled high in a bowl for spoonin' and rich cream in glass quart bottles for pouring. There was enough for helpings all around and then some.

Folks inside the house were smiling and lickin' their lips, smelling the honey glaze and the fresh roast coffee while waiting for the festivities to start.

Outside was a different matter.

Cars and pickups were still puttering into the Delphi Falls from the front gate like a Memorial Day parade, parking any which way. Must have been about twenty or so.

"I wonder who's coming," Big Mike said.

The look on his face was a hint he was in on a secret. People lined up waiting to get in the house. It was Mike Shea and the sheriff they let in first. Most behind them edged their way in and smelled the coffee and donuts. They gathered about, most removing their hats and waiting for proper introductions and invites.

Sheriff Hood looked out the front window to the end of the long drive where he could see Dick driving in, Duba behind him in the pickup, and then Conway in his Chevy.

"They're here," Sheriff Hood said. "We can start when they come in."

They parked in front of the barn garage and a group of gents and two young ladies crawled out of their vehicles and followed the lads into the house.

As they came in, the sheriff directed them to come stand with him.

"Would you folks please stand over here?"

He pointed toward the upright piano against the wall.

Little did he or anyone else know ole Charlie here and Sir Arthur Conan Doyle were setting on top of the upright, taking it all in.

Big Mike got people's attention. He had a sense the sheriff was ready and had something important to say.

"Thank you all for being here," Sheriff Hood said. "You may not know each other, but many of you folks are here because you were pickpocketed at the state fair. Some came because you helped us catch the culprit...and, yes, he is behind bars today. But I'll let Mike Shea take it from here."

Big Mike interjected, "Farmer and Mrs. Parker are here to say goodbye to our new friend, Flying Eddie. But we hope it's only a short while when we see him again. We think the Parkers want to adopt him."

Mike Shea stepped up.

"I'm happy to report that persons who were robbed at the state fair have received their money and wallets or their purses back. I know most of you, and it pleases me to see you came for some fellowship and glazed donuts, compliments of Big Mike and Missus."

"Already?" Mary asked.

"Already what, Mary?" Mike Shea asked.

"Everybody got their money back already?"

"Yes," Mike Shea said. "Well, they either have it, or they know we have it and will get it to them."

"Wow, how to go guys," Mary said.

"Fortunately, we were able to identify the owners of the wallets and purses and most of them were at home last night."

Mike Shea pointed to the young people standing by the piano.

"Those young folks over by the piano are all performers in the Sherlock Holmes Play."

"Where's the play?" came a voice.

"The play is going on this afternoon and tonight up in New Woodstock."

"At the school?"

"Yes."

"But they're the crooks, aren't they?" a voice asked.

"They knew nothing of the pickpocket's shenanigans," Sheriff Hood said. "They were surprised by it. He was an actor with them, and they were disappointed to hear what he had done."

"So, he was Sherlock Holmes?" Duba asked.

"The best," one of the actors said.

"He was their lead actor," Mike Shea said.

"He's in the pokey?"

"Yes," Sheriff Hood said.

"They have what's called an understudy who can play his part," Mike Shea said.

"What I would like you to know is it was those actors standing over there that called you folks last night or drove to your homes and returned the wallets and purses before midnight and apologized for their friend's error in his ways," Sheriff Hood said.

"Was it hard finding the places, your being from England?" Holbrook asked.

The eldest Sherlock Holmes player answered.

"Someone who knew the area went with each of us, mate."

"That was smart," Mary said.

"The hardest part was driving on the proper side of the road. We do it differently back home."

"Thievery it was," mumbled one farmer.

214

"It certainly was," Mike Shea said. "Several pressed charges against the scoundrel last night."

"Being as there were charges pressed," Sheriff Hood said, "I called Mike Shea to see if we could get a court date set. The law says the young man has to go before a judge."

"Folks, I called Judge Munson in Syracuse late last night," Mike Shea said. "I woke him up, in fact. I told him the situation we had and asked him about setting a court date, given the extenuating circumstance that the pickpocket isn't a citizen."

"We wanted to take his confessing into consideration," Sheriff Hood said. "The fact he wanted to make restitution."

Mike Shea added, "I told Judge Munson about the acting company calling you folks and the others and apologizing on behalf of their friend—and of getting wallets and purses they could, back to their owners—one even being as far away as Schenectady."

"He needs to pay for his crime," came a voice.

"And he will," the sheriff said.

"Judge Munson met us in the courthouse at two this morning," Mike Shea said. "His bailiff showed up in his pajamas. The court reporter came in hair curlers. But we sure enough had a court. The young man pled guilty. He didn't hide behind excuses."

"We told the judge how the money was returned, or the owners notified—and that's all we told him, I assure you," the sheriff said. "It wasn't our intent to go light on him."

"Judge Munson gave him ninety days, at which time he's deported and has to leave the country," the sheriff said. "He's letting him serve his time in Cazenovia's city jail."

"Good," a voice from the crowd said.

"Serves him right," another said.

With the air cleared about the capture and punishment of the notorious pickpocket, Big Mike called Eddie up to the table for the first glazed donut and cup of coffee.

"Eddie," Big Mike said, "we are proud to have made your acquaintance. You've only been here a week, but you've graced us with a week we'll be talking about for a long time."

"You gave us an adventure we'll never forget," Tall Jerry said.

"Thank you from all of us and special thanks for your service to our country, especially on D-Day," Missus said.

"You'll have many friends here, Eddie," Mary said.

The gathering was abuzz after that. Folks going about socializing and catching up with each other while licking the glaze chips from their lip and sipping coffee or hot chocolate. It was a time.

It was round about the second cup Big Mike took Eddie aside and told him to call a Mr. Spaulding when he got back to Binghamton. Mr. Spaulding owned a bakery in Binghamton and was a friend of Big Mike. Said he would give Eddie a job—any job he wanted—and he'd let him off to give plane rides at the state fair, as well.

Eddie stepped over and asked Barber to gather the book club around for some last words. They came with a warm glazed donut in their hands.

"I don't know what to say other than you're the best friends a body could have."

"We all love you, Eddie," Mary said.

"I'm sorry I was such a mess when I got here."

"You survived and you didn't kill us," Marty said. "We're even."

"Thank you for helping me through it…and I hope you think of me as a friend."

"When you land in Binghamton, park that plane fast and run and give hugs," Mary said.

"You can count on it."

"Hug them for us, too," Mary said.

"Eddie, don't be landing on top of any hayfield hills or too close to barns. We'll want to see you back here in one piece," Dick said.

Randy saluted Eddie. "Thanks for the ride in your plane, Eddie."

Then he teared up and turned away.

It was before the third cup the Sherlock Holmes Players let it slip they had free tickets for anyone who wanted to go to the show.

"What good would a play about Sherlock Holmes be without Sherlock Holmes in it?" Farmer Clancy from up the hill near the hamlet asked.

"Farmer Clancy, the young man is in jail, serving his time at the moment," Sheriff Hood said.

"He can't be in the play," Mike Shea said.

"What good is a Sherlock Holmes play without Sherlock Holmes being in it?" Farmer Clancy repeated.

"Farmer Clancy, what are you saying? Are you saying they shouldn't have the play?"

"Well..."

"They have a substitute actor for the Sherlock Holmes role," Mike Shea said.

"I'm suggesting just because the varmint inconvenienced us once ain't no reason he should be allowed to get away with inconveniencing us agin' by not acting in the play that people like us paid good money to see, is all," Farmer Clancy argued.

"He's right," a voice said.

"We didn't pay all that money just to see a substitute," Farmer Clancy said.

"Farmer Clancy, you didn't pay for tickets," Mike Shea said.

"What's your point, Mike?" Farmer Clancy grunted.

"The tickets all of you have were given to you free of charge by these actor folks," Mike Shea said.

"Makes no never mind," Farmer Clancy insisted.

"Excuse me?" Mike Shea asked.

"A play just ain't a play of any quality without, well, you know— the players."

"Farmer Clancy, might I remind you that you were the one who pressed charges against the lad?"

"Well, what's that got to do with a play?"

"Yeah!" chorused the second and third persons who pressed charges against the pickpocket. "What's that got to do with the play?"

"I say give him back some of his own medicine," Farmer Clancy said.

"Just what do you have in mind?" the sheriff asked.

"He took something that didn't belong to him. Make him give us something that does—a free performance."

Farmer Clancy's proposition was a compelling conflict in local jurisprudence was how Sir Arthur Conan Doyle put it to ole Charlie here.

Mrs. Clancy interrupted, hoping to put it all to rest.

"You're not going to win, Sheriff. Rick's pretty much made up his mind. His favorite book—one he keeps at the bedside is Sherlock Holmes. The only reason he pressed charges was the rapscallion besmirched the name of Sherlock Holmes. Weren't no other reason t'all."

"Is this right, Farmer Clancy?" the sheriff asked.

"Rick Clancy, you tell the sheriff like it is now," Mrs. Clancy said.

Clancy stood stiff and tight-mouthed. His lips were sealed.

"Show of hands," the sheriff said. "How many here want to see the Sherlock Holmes play with Sherlock Holmes in it?"

Hands went up.

"And how many will watch it without resorting to the temptations of booing or hissing or throwing grapefruits or rotten tomatoes?" Mike Shea asked.

Every hand but Farmer Clancy's stayed up.

"Rick, you're objecting?" the sheriff asked, befuddled.

"When will his ninety days start, Sheriff—yesterday, today, or tomorrow after the show?"

"How about tomorrow," Sheriff Hood said. "After the shows this afternoon and tonight. Will that suit you?"

Clancy's arm went full up.

Pots and urns emptied, donuts gone, folks walked together down the driveway and to the field just beyond the alfalfa field.

"Farmer Parker, Mrs. Parker," Eddie whispered. "When I get her in the air, watch for my wave. It'll be just for you. I'm sorry I was such a nuisance. Thank you both for being so generous with me. I'll bring the family by soon, I promise."

The book club followed Eddie across the field to his plane.

"We're standing here at the end of the runway so we can wave when you take off and fly over us," Mary said.

Flying Eddie started her up, moved the chocks and taxied down the length of the field. Everyone but the book club members were lined up along the road.

From a distance you could hear the engine roaring as he turned the plane around to take off, the propeller slicing through the air, pistons pounding. The biplane rolled and bumped along the length of the field getting bigger and bigger, the faster she came.

Just before it jumped off the ground and into the air, Eddie looked out the side of his cockpit, caught Mary's eye, pointed to her, saluted and off he flew.

Up it jumped, over the trees next to the creek, climbing up Farmer Parker's side pasture hill and Buddy's grave. The plane disappeared over the hill.

It was just as people started milling about when the plane reappeared, going the wrong way. Engine whining as it sliced the air flying fighter-plane fast at a low thousand feet to the Maxwell place down on the corner. Once there it banked a sweeping U turn roll and sped back, straight as an arrow up Cardner Road.

Farmer and Mrs. Parker were in the middle of the road waving at the lad. At just the right moment the wings of the plane did a sharp tip down to the right and up and then a sharp tip down to the left and up.

It was an Air Force salute to the Parkers, Flying Eddie's new friends.

The plane climbed, passing the Delphi Falls on its left and disappearing over Farmer Parker's pasture hill and into a cloud in the horizon, on its way home to Binghamton…

EPILOGUE

I'm inclined to think globalization had its roots just prior to 1939, with the advent of the first and only global world war this planet has ever known. If we take the time to remember this war and the times—study it, not bury it—the world just might learn how to coexist. Look at the largest war in history that ripped our world apart, and you'll agree it was our ability to coexist during those horrendous years that enabled the world to ultimately prevail and win the war. If we don't keep a lamp burning and retain the history of WWII for other generations to study, the Hitlers of hatred will win in time.

Jerome Mark Antil